What Can a Pot Say About a Kettle?

A Play

by Craig Anthony Attaway

RoseDog🐾Books
PITTSBURGH, PENNSYLVANIA 15238

RoseDog Books
585 Alpha Drive, Suite 103
Pittsburgh, PA 15238
Visit our website at *www.rosedogbookstore.com*

ISBN: 978-1-4809-8121-8
eISBN: 978-1-4809-8098-3

Cast of Characters

Zharquaviyont, *LuPearl's gay son*
Becky Lynn, *friend of Zharquaviyont and Paula's daughter*
LuPearl, *Zharquaviyont and Franklin's mother*
Franklin Potts III, *Zharquaviyont's brother*
Ida, *friend of Becky Lynn and Zharquaviyont*
Paula, *Becky Lynn's mother*

Scene 1

In the opening scene LuPearl and Zharquaviyont (with earbuds in at all times) take the stage. They have just returned from the funeral home. Zharquaviyont is wearing an LGBTQ T-shirt in rainbow colors and a pair of yellow pants, size 4. LuPearl was designated by her ex-husband Col. Frank Potts, years prior to their divorce, to be executor of his last will and testament. Ida and Becky Lynn, Zharquaviyont's two best friends from high school, arrive soon thereafter. Their dialogue begins off stage. After Ida and Becky Lynn enter, they all approach the sofa, sit and share a blanket. Ida is texting the entire time. Someone snaps a "selfie" every five or so minutes.

Zharquaviyont:
You haven't heard from Frank to come and pick him up from the airport yet, Momma? His plane shoulda landed two and a half hours ago. I'm so done with him.

LuPearl begins to tidy up the house and says:
No, baby, he hasn't called me yet, he probably had a layover in Dallas. No matter where you're goin'…child, you'll always have a layover in Dallas. He'll be callin' any minute now, I'm sure. Donovan hadn't called yet either. I don't know what gets into your brothers sometimes.

Zharquaviyont receives a text. After responding and taking a selfie he says:
Well, Momma, they're your kids.

LuPearl:
And your derned brothers.

LuPearl and Zharquaviyont share a laugh at an inside family joke.

Zharquaviyont:
Now Momma, I know you've got another migraine. So don't come in here and get busy cleaning up. I'll clean up the house. You take half of your pill and just lay on down and rest…alright? I'll keep the noise down while you take your nap. Funeral arrangements are difficult to make.

LuPearl:
It sure puts a lot on your mind. But yeah. I think I will go and try to lie down for a few hours.

Zharquaviyont:
Yes, ma'am. Sleep well, Momma. I love you.

LuPearl:

Not as much as I love you, baby. Not as much as I love you.

> **After LuPearl hugs Zharquaviyont for approximately three seconds, turns and climbs to the top of the stairs, the doorbell rings.**

Zharquaviyont:

Who is it?

> **Becky Lynn answers from the other side of the door.**

Becky Lynn:

Qua-Qua...it's us. *Common sense!*

Zharquaviyont:

Child, who is "us"? "Us" could be anybody! I don't let strangers into my Momma's house!

Becky Lynn:

Qua-Qua, open the door.

> **Zharquaviyont answers the door, allowing Becky Lynn and Ida to enter. As they enter, they take turns exchanging "pretend kissed on the cheek" with Zharquaviyont. Ida is wearing a football jersey with number 7 on front and back.**

Ida:

What's up, Fam?!

Zharquaviyont:

Heyyyyyy, birthday girl. Kiss, kiss.

Becky Lynn:

Qua…I sent you a message from my new account. Why didn't you like me back?

Zharquaviyont:

Girl, I just got back from the funeral home with Momma. She was given the responsibility of making the arrangements for her ex-husband, Colonel Potts.

Becky Lynn:

Oh. Okay. I didn't know. I'm sorry.

Zharquaviyont:

Don't be sorry. There's no way you could have known.

Ida:

Can you guys believe that we're about to be high school graduates? It's gonna feel so weird walking across the stage to shake sweaty Mr. Faulkner's hand. He was always sooooo creepy. Both he and his unibrow make my skin crawl.

Becky Lynn:

Qua-Qua, I'm sorry that your brothers didn't make it in for your hair show de-but.

Ida:
That's de-bue. It's pronounced de-bue. It's not de-but. You're so basic.

**Becky Lynn is a freckled-faced fiery redhead girl
with an uncontrollable head of hair. It's a constant
struggle for her. She stands at 5' 3" tall and is more
than ample 36-24-36:**

Uh…excuse me…was I speaking to you? No, I didn't think so. (pause)
Anyway…as I was saying…that must have been hard for you not to have
them here. How long has it been since your brothers have been home?

Zharquaviyont:
It's been a whole minute. A little bit more than five months for Donovan and for Frank, well over three years. Donovan is stationed in Italy
and Frank goes to military college in another state. "Mr. Ultra-macho."
He gets on my last nerve…believe you me! He only comes home for
funerals. This time…his own father has passed. I can't stand him.

Ida:
Qua-Qua…you sound salty AF right now. Why are you throwing shade
on your own brother?

Zharquaviyont:
Uh…this ain't shade, honey. This is facts. He always wants to do everything better than everybody else…always tryin' to outdo somebody.
With him…honey, everything is a competition. He'll compete with
anybody in anything. Franklin is the kind of person who has an exten-
sive plan for everything he does. And I do mean *every…single…thing.*

Ida:

You say something like that every day. Why are you so worried about people outdoing you? That's a sad way to live Qua...real talk. Can your self-esteem *get* any lower?

Zharquaviyont puts his left hand to his chest and says:

Uh...excuse you? (repeat with a dramatic pause) Don't get snatched up out of your feelings up in here, boo-boo. The fuse is shorter than usual today. I'm telling you up front.

Becky Lynn:

There's nothing wrong with future planning, Qua-Qua. *That's goals.* Planning ahead is *very* important. *Common sense.*

Zharquaviyont:

Child...His future plan has fifteen steps to it. No sane person makes *with fifteen steps.* Prime example...my oldest brother, Donovan, enlisted right after high school and has done fine...but Frank? Noooo. Frank decided to go through ROTC and be commissioned as a *Second Lieutenant.* Reason being? (pause) Just so that he would outrank Donovan. Frank's problem is that he's too much like his daddy. He was a military officer, too. *Colonel Frank Potts II.*

Zharquaviyont gives both a sarcastic and feminine salute with his left hand.

Ida:

Show some respect for the deceased.

Becky Lynn:
His dad?

Zharquaviyont:
Yeah. Same mother, different fathers. My brothers and I don't look anything alike. Donovan has always been on the chubby side no matter what he did. Frank is 6' 4", 225 pounds, and then there's yours truly. 5' 2", 122 pounds of magnificence, baby…okay?

High fives and finger snaps are exchanged.

Donovan is Donovan Hampton Jr., Frank is Franklin Potts III, and I am the one and only…drumroll, please?

The two girls begin an impromptu and pacifying drumroll.

Zharquaviyont:
Zharquaviyont Zebedee Lacy, baby…Heyyyyyyy! Baby, that's three snaps in a "Z"…two for you and one for me!

Ida:
I can't imagine what that must be like. My parents were high school sweethearts and have been married for like…forever or something like that.

Becky Lynn pretends to applaud and speaks sarcastically:
And we're so happy for you, Ida.

Ida:
Excuse me. Was I speaking to you? *Was I speaking to you?! I didn't think so.*

Both speak simultaneously.

Becky Lynn:
We already know that you grew up with both parents in the home. Okay? You don't have to keep goin' on and on about it. *We get it!*

Ida:
Anyway…anyway…you're so *trailer park. You can take the T.H.O.T. out of the trailer park but you can't take the trailer park out of the T.H.O.T.*

Ida repeatedly makes a gesture in Becky Lynn's face for her to stop speaking.

Ida:
Shhhhh! Qua-Qua's mother is trying to sleep. Show some respect. Don't you have any home training at all?

Becky Lynn:
Don't put your hand in my face. Who knows where that hand has been? And the only T.H.O.T. here is you.

Ida turns her back on Becky Lynn with her left index finger extended:

No, no, no (pause), no. Anyway (pause) Qua-Qua…what's that on your chest?

Zharquaviyont takes his hand, exposes his bare chest, and says:
Sexiness. (three-second pause) Oh, you mean this Band-Aid? Child, I

donated blood today. My chest was where they found the best vein. You guys should come with me next time. They pay you for your plasma.

Ida:

I'm afraid of needles and I'm not too crazy about the sight of blood. But thank you very much.

Becky Lynn sarcastically:

Girl, you'd better go on and get that free AIDS test.

Ida:

What did you just say to me, *PUTA*!? El pez por su boca muere. (The fish will die through his mouth.)

Becky Lynn:

I don't know what you said but we're just playin'. Don't be calling me out of my name. And use English when you speak to me. Anyway, Qua-Qua, you do know that having different fathers is no big deal, right? It's just the way the world works. You already know that my twin sister and I have a half-sister. But rewind a little bit. You haven't seen your own brother in *three years?* And your brother Donovan...where is he?

Zharquaviyont:

He's in Italy on some base close to Pordenone. We're all on social media but yeah, he was home about five months ago. But as for Frank...he's almost like a stranger to us. I would never say this in front of Momma but he thinks he's too good for us.

Ida:

Man, that's hella messed up.

Zharquaviyont:

You wanna hear messed up? Honey…whenever he's around…little old me becomes *invisible*. Frank this and Frank that. Everything is about Frank Potts. That's my brother and I love him but I can't stand him. I'm serious. And while we're on the subject of messed up, Becky Lynn… what's going on with your hair?

Becky Lynn puts both hands on top of her head and says:

Shut up. What's wrong with my hair?!

Zharquaviyont:

Child, where would I even begin? It's wild. Assume the position, honey. *Assume the position.*

Becky Lynn gets up from the sofa and takes a seat on the floor between Zharquaviyont's legs. After she does so, he begins brushing her hair with a brush from her bag. Ida mockingly applauds, gets up from the sofa, walks behind, and then begins to style Zharquaviyont's hair.

Zharquaviyont:

What are you supposed to be clappin' for?! That cap's not hiding anything. You don't have any room to talk, honey. Believe you me.

Becky Lynn:

I know, right?! (pause) Qua-Qua, after biology class I thought maybe you took a while to go home. But I was wrong because your truck was gone. The parking lot that you usually park in was empty. So I reported back to class "sad and glue me," whatever that means.

Ida:

The word is gloomy! G-L-O-O-M-Y. It means dismayed or pessimistic. What did you even have to do to even get to the 12th grade? *Somebody* must've put in some work!

Becky Lynn:

And you have the nerve to talk about home training? Anyway…Qua… I came out there hoping to see you talk. I owe you an apology.

Zharquaviyont:

What are you talking about?! I get so sick of you sayin' "I'm sorry" all the time. An apology for what, Becky Lynn? You're always apologizing to everybody.

Ida:

I know, right?

Zharquaviyont:

Stop being so extra. Why are you always so apologetic all of the time anyway?

Ida:

Don't look for fangs in the mouth of a free horse, Qua-Qua. Tell me something. If holy water was packaged, shipped, and sold in forty-ounce bottles, would that be offensive? Why or why not?

Zharquaviyont:

Ida…you're doin' too much. Question, though. What are you on and how can I get some?

Ida:

I'm asking a serious philosophical question here about advertising and marketing. I'm thinking about majoring in International Business.

Zharquaviyont:

Again…what are you on and how can I get some? I mean…fangs in the mouth of a free horse? Holy water in forty-ounce bottles? What in the world are *you* talking about?!

Ida:

If holy water was packaged, shipped, and sold in forty-ounce bottles, would it be offensive?

Zharquaviyont:

Yes, that would be offensive! Have you lost your mind? How could you even come up with a question like that?

Becky Lynn claps her hands five times, turns around, and says:

Qua-Qua…stay focused. She just wants attention. Ignore her idle chatter and useless rhetoric.

Ida:

Useless rhetoric?! Ahhhhhhhh, listen to that! Somebody has overheard somebody else using a big word or two. *You go with your vocabulary, girrrrrl.*

Becky Lynn turns back around and says:

Qua-Qua, I owe you an apology for how I acted in the cafeteria. I had no reason to snap on you and I hope you'll please forgive me. I seem to be getting upset *for no reason* lately. I hope you understand and live with it as long as I do it. Because…what I'm trying to say…is that I love you very much and that I don't want to lose you as my friend.

Zharquaviyont:

Sounds like a personal problem. Could we please postpone the Becky Lynn show for right now? I'm really not in the mood for this drama. Um already stressin' out about that boy coming home. Stop apologizing so much…please! It's hella aggravating.

Becky Lynn:

Hold on, let me finish. You always try to do everything to make a person happy and feel loved. You don't hide your feelings. I've never had anyone to treat me as good as you have. I don't think I'll ever find another person who is as good as you are.

> **Ida makes violin playing motions and pretends to trace a tear down her cheek.**

Zharquaviyont:

Girl, ain't nobody thinking 'boutchu! That's why I didn't clap back. I know when your cycle starts…Ida's too. Honey, I just chalked it up to hormonal imbalance. Okay? Okay.

Ida:

Qua…now *you're doing too much. You're doin' too much.*

Zharquaviyont:

And another thing…you both may wanna reconsider taking those birth control pills? They do more than just control birth. They can also regulate your periods.

Becky Lynn:

I know that! Nobody's even talkin' about that. And birth control pills make your butt and your breast too big. I'm not tryin to do that. That reminds me, Ida...I have some things for you. Qua...would you hand her that vinegar and water solution and deodorant stick from my bag, please?

Zharquaviyont:

Becky Lynn, you really don't have any room to talk. As tight as your jeans are...you're gonna give yourself a yeast infection.

Ida:

Solo el que carga el costal sabe l que lleva dentro. (Only he that carries the sack knows what's inside.) What a hypocrite. I'm actually about to vomit.

Becky Lynn:

You're like another sister to me. Don't be offended...I'm just trying to help you keep fresh. Us girls have to stick together, you know. I'll even open it for you.

> **Becky Lynn removes the exterior deodorant cap and struggles to remove the interior cap with her teeth. After approximately ten seconds of Ida and Zharquaviyont looking back and forth toward each other, Zharquaviyont reaches for the deodorant and says:**

Zharquaviyont:

You don't pull that with your teeth...you just roll it up. Observe. **Zhar-**

quaviyont rolls the deodorant stick upward. Oh, and Ida? (pointing toward Ida's hair) We need to schedule some time so that we can take care of whatever that is you've got goin' on up there. Okay? Okay.

Ida snarls her upper lip:
Whatever! I'm snatched *and* an athlete. I don't have to worry about my hair.

Becky Lynn laughing:
Didn't expect the clap back, did you? (pause) And that's not the only thing you don't worry about.

Ida:
My man likes it.

Zharquaviyont:
And there it is! There it is! What's it been, about a hot two minutes?

Ida, with her palms up:
What?!

Becky Lynn:
Qua-Qua and I bet $20 that you couldn't have a conversation without talking about your triflin' boyfriend. Because of you…I owe him another $20.

> **Becky Lynn reaches into her bag and hands Zhar-quaviyont a twenty-dollar bill.**

Ida:
Sounds like envy to me. Esemiga celosa! (Jealous hater!) No soy mone-

dita de oro para caerles bien a todos. (I am not a golden coin so not everybody will like me.) Don't hate 'cause you can't get dates.

Becky Lynn:
Whatever! I'm goin' broke gambling on you and I'm trying to be supportive.

Zharquaviyont:
MyKurtys, MyKurtys, MyKurtys. I'm *soooo* done hearing about MyKurtys Dixon! What kinda name is MyKurtys anyway? M-Y-K-U-R-T-Y-S. Why not just Curtis? C-U-R-T-I-S.

Becky Lynn covers her mouth as she laughs.

Ida:
When he was born, his mother said, "This is my Curtis." And that became his name. He complains when I go to church, always likes to run the streets, go to parties and stay out half the next day. When we get into arguments, he goes out and gets drunk and wants to hit on me. Other than that, he lies constantly until I never know when he's telling the truth. He doesn't want to help with the baby and denies her when he gets mad and he always asking for a blood test. And when I offered him one, he didn't want to take it!

MyKurtys Dixon is a prime example of the privileged quarterback who has been taught, from the time that he was six years old, that he was more important than everyone else. The rules of society have never applied to him. He has received exceedingly special treatment because of his athletic abil-

ities. Each and every one of his coaches have profited from his abilities and so has he. As long as he continues to line pockets...he will continue to be the epitome of ghetto elitism. His worst days are yet to come.

Zharquaviyont:

Child, you were supposed to get all of your horseplay, foolishness and nonsense out of your system in your sophomore year, not your senior year. I tried to tell you that he was sus to begin with. You could do *soooooooo* much better than him. Who buys the baby's diapers and stuff?!

Ida:

His mom...my parents and me. I've spent money on him but he won't spend money on me. The only time he'll help with the baby is when I threaten to leave or make him pay child support. *I told him* that I could find someone else to take care of my needs *and help me with my baby.* If it weren't for my family helping me through school, I don't know what I would've done. I would leave him...if I didn't love him so much. Anyway...what kinda name is Zharquaviyont?!

Zharquaviyont:

Wuda, cuda, shuda. Don't change the subject. And Zharquaviyont is normal, *thank you!* Anyway, how many times can you break up and get back together with a fool?! You can have any guy at our school! After the way he treats you...*girl, why are you still with him?!*

Ida:

Because I love him!

Zharquaviyont:

All you do is argue every day. The only reason that your father and brothers haven't clicked on him is because your mom won't allow it. How can you love someone who hits you?!

Ida:

Silly boy, you're so oblivious. Don't you know…that you can't get to the makeup without the breakup? *That's my boo-thing!* And believe me, making up gets better and better every time. The last time…it felt like he grew a couple of inches and got thicker. Ooooooh, girl, change the subject. I'm trying to get excited! But that's a different conversation. *You know my boo-thing is about to announce which football scholarship he's gonna accept next year, right?*

Becky Lynn:

What? You didn't tell us about that. (five-second pause) So Ida…what's MyKurtys workin' with?

Ida:

Excuse me?!

Becky Lynn:

What I said…

Ida:

Excuse me?!

Becky Lynn:

What I said…

Ida:

Oh, I heard what you said! But I'm going to sit and pretend that I didn't hear you just ask me what my man is working with! You know what? I'm cool. It's all good…no need to get turnt.

Ida looks to Zharquaviyont and says:

Qua-Qua, I apologize. I'm sorry for disrespecting your mom's house.

Becky Lynn shrugs her shoulders with her palms facing up and says:

Well…you're always bragging about him. I just thought I'd ask what he was packin'…that's all.

Ida:

Well, now you've asked. Alright? Move on.

Becky Lynn:

But you didn't answer me.

Ida:

Well…let me put it like this, boo-boo. He's got all he's supposed to have and a whole bunch of somebody else's. Okay? If it's not magnum…he can't wear it, baby. And if you don't want to have to fight in *your condition*…I suggest you drop it.

Zharquaviyont:

Condition? What condition?

Becky Lynn ignores the question:

Okay. Who knows? Maybe I will drop it.

Zharquaviyont:
What condition?

Becky Lynn "drops it to the floor" and stands back up three times. Ida gets angry and points her finger into Becky Lynn's face:
See…you play too much. You play too much! That's the problem with a T.H.O.T., T.H.O.T.s don't know how to keep their mouths shut.

Becky Lynn:
Nuttin' between us but air and opportunity, Chica. Nuttin' but air and opportunity.

Zharquaviyont whispers sternly:
Hey…hey…hey. Don't disrespect my Momma's house. Didn't you just apologize, Ida? You know she's just playin'. You know that she's a master at pushin' people's buttons. Calm it down.

Becky Lynn:
Really? Just like always, you're gonna take her side?

Zharquaviyont:
I'm not takin anybody's side. Honey, I'm completely neutral. And I'd just like to tell both of you in neutral way to calm down or get put out. What say you?

Becky Lynn puts her palms up in a surrendering manner and says:
I'm cool. She's the one you should be asking that question, not me.

Zharquaviyont:
If I'm looking at you…I'm talking to you. Be cool or be gone. What's it gonna be?

Becky Lynn:

I'll apologize if she will.

Zharquaviyont:

Ida, it's all on you. Make a decision.

Ida composes herself:

As I've already stated, I apologize for disrespecting your mother's home.

Becky Lynn:

So, MyKurtys is going to announce his college choice, huh? It's about time something exciting happened around here…boring day and night. When night comes nothing changes. It's just a lot darker than the day.

Ida:

The real problem here is that you just don't know how to have fun. But anyway, MyKurtys said that it's gonna be either Florida or California! That just means I'll have to learn how to surf?!

Becky Lynn:

You'll have to learn how to surf?! That's what you get for having a younger boyfriend. You're the class valedictorian. Are you really gonna wait around here another year just for *him* to graduate? Common sense.

Ida:

I go where he goes. Wherever I go, I'll be at the top academically speaking. And if they have a soccer team…it's a wrap. Check this out. I've been a varsity soccer player since I got here. *Am I right or wrong?*

Ida is the most phenomenal soccer player that the school has ever seen...male or female. She is a scoring machine. Becky Lynn and Zharquaviyont speaking simultaneously:
Yes, Ida.

Ida:
And I'm gonna be the class valedictorian hands down with the 4.5 GPA, right?

Becky Lynn and Zharquaviyont:
Yes, Ida.

Ida:
Then you already know I'm calling the shots! I'm gonna work at my parents' restaurant for one more year...keep stacking racks on top of racks before I go off to college. What's up with your plans, Becky Lynn? It must really hurt to know that your twin sister is going away to college and you're not. What have you decided to do?

Becky Lynn:
Still undecided, thanks for asking.

Zharquaviyont:
Where is Nicole going to college again, Becky Lynn?

Becky Lynn:
I don't know...somewhere in Texas on a cheerleading scholarship. A cheerleading scholarship?! Seriously?! I didn't even know there *was* such a thing but Nicole is *all into cheerleading now*. She was really second alternate, but the first alternate quit and later one of the cheerleaders

quit. That was a break for her and I wish someone would give me a break!

Ida:
It may sound strange to you, but for people who really want to succeed… they do whatever they have to. What about you, Qua-Qua? What are you gonna do now that we're practically graduates?

Zharquaviyont:
Girl, I don't know if college is in my future either. Even though Mrs. Hughes says that I'm the best student she's ever had…the only class I excel in is cosmetology. One of my brothers is already in the military, the other is well on his way to becoming an officer in the military and here I am…cosmetology boy. I do hair and push cuticles back…that's it.

Becky Lynn:
Stop putting yourself down…I hate it when you do that! You don't have to follow in your brother's footsteps or anyone else's. Just do you. Maybe you could take some business classes and own your own salon. You could charge the other stylists booth rental fees.

Zharquaviyont:
That's what's up! See? That's why you're my girl! I've never even thought about that. It would be like I was landlord or something like that, right?

Becky Lynn:
That's right. *Common sense!*

Zharquaviyont:

Honey…you're using your go-to phrase a little too much today. Okay? Hearing "Common sense" every five seconds is getting on my nerves… boo-boo. You're getting on my nerves.

Ida:

I know, right? Find another catch phrase. (pause) Qua-Qua, have you ever even *thought* of joining the military? It could be a whole new opportunity in life. There must be something that you already like to do that you would do for free. What else do you enjoy doing?

> **Zharquaviyont looks at Ida in a peculiar way and snaps his fingers once.**

Ida:

Something other than that! C'mon, be serious. What do you like doing?

Zharquaviyont:

Nuttin' really. Girl, I can't be in no military. I'm not cut out for rules and regulations. All of that marchin'…and cutting my hair? And having somebody standin' and yelling *in my face*? Oh, but no. (pause) But then again…I could get used to being around all them soldiers in uniform, baby! Three snaps in a Z!

> **Zharquaviyont snaps his fingers in a circular motion.**

Ida:

People don't go into the military to meet guys, Qua.

Zharquaviyont:

Says you, honey…says you.

Ida receives another text. Zharquaviyont says to Becky Lynn:

That's what you get when you speak of the devil. Becky Lynn…I'm gonna give you a chance to win your money back. I'll bet you $60 it's MyKurtys Dixon blowin' her phone up her right now.

Becky Lynn:

You already have too much of my money thanks to Ida. Our betting days are over. Believe that.

Ida checks her phone and says:

It's him. He wants to know where I am. He should already know that. I'm always with you guys.

Becky Lynn:

Really, Ida? Like seriously? Don't tell him where you are. He doesn't have to know your moment to moment whereabouts. You don't belong to him and you should be your own person. *Common sense!*

Ida:

Yeah…but **what can a pot say about a kettle**…Detroit?

Zharquaviyont:

Girl, you know good and well that she's gonna tell him where she is. MyKurtys Dixon is just like Frank. He can't keep his pants up either. They *know* Frank is a dog and they just love him to death. He specifically goes after girls who have been dropped by their boyfriends after they've had a baby. He calls them *easy pickens*…works every time.

Ida:

Is that your way of throwing shade my way? What are you really trying to say?

Zharquaviyont:

You know me…I don't throw shade and I always keep it a huned (100). And by the by, Becky Lynn…Detroit was always suspect, too.

Ida:

Don't try to change the subject, Qua. I think that I already know what you're trying to say but go ahead. Don't go on hush-mouth now.

Becky Lynn:

Common sense. He's trying to say that MyKurtys specifically chose you because you already had a baby. He doesn't care anything about you. He's just using you to get his swerve on.

Zharquaviyont:

Don't put words in my mouth, Becky Lynn…thank you very much. Ida…real talk. Everybody says that that baby looks like Rodney. I wasn't there so I don't know. All I'm saying is that most girls who already have a child with "guy A" are more than anxious to jump into a (**Zharquaviyont uses air quotes**) relationship with "guy B" especially if "guy A" is no longer in the picture. That's all I'm saying.

Becky Lynn:

Well, I guess that a piece of a relationship is better than no relationship at all, right?

Zharquaviyont:

That's a straight-up lie. A piece of a relationship is the same thing as no relationship at all. Ida...honey, you're in a P.O.M. relationship. Go off to college and study International Business and leave us and that buster behind. That's what you need to do.

Ida:

Who are you to tell me what I need to do? What are you gonna to do?

Becky Lynn:

What's that supposed to mean actually? A P.O.M. relationship?

Zharquaviyont:

Ida...I'm only telling you this *because I love you like a sister.* A P.O.M. relationship is a Piece of Meat relationship with nothing more than a sperm donor. He's a piece of meat for you and you're a piece of meat for him. You deserve so much better than him.

Ida:

Really, Qua? Did you really just say that to me?

Ida receives and reads another text from MyKurtys and then hands her cell phone to Becky Lynn. Becky Lynn reads aloud: "Does your daddy know you're gonna b naughty 2night?"

> **Becky Lynn hands the phone back to Ida, who begins texting. When she is finished, she hands the phone to Becky Lynn again and Becky Lynn reads it aloud.**

Becky Lynn:

"Hope you have a place picked out where we can b and won't b disturbed or n a hurry. I like 2take my time. But if it can't b helped, it won't make it any worse on me to hurry but u just might not b finished. Besides, the feelings last a long time afterwards, if u know what I mean."

Zharquaviyont:

My stomach just flipped and I think I may throw up. In the van, in the park, on the ground or just wherever, right? Ida, you're a straight-A student and he probably just robbed a gas station. *What's the attraction? I mean.* Have you ever considered the number of girls who've been in his van before and/or since you? Have you ever thought about that?

Becky Lynn tosses the phone back to Ida in disgust. Zharquaviyont claps his hands once and begins to chant and dance. Becky Lynn joins in:

"Ida Dixon, that's ya name. Ida Dixon, that's ya name. Ida Dixon, that's ya name. Ida Dixon, that's ya name. Ida Dixon, that's ya name." Ida Dixon, that's ya name.

Ida simultaneously:

Really? You're both so juvenile. You guys really need to grow up, you know? Why do I even continue to hang out with you two losers?

Becky Lynn:

Qua-Qua? Remember that other boyfriend song?

Becky Lynn claps her hands once and they both chant and dance:

Coxy Jean, Coxy Jean, Coxy Jean, Coxy Jean, Coxy Jean.

Ida:

Hello? Qua-Qua. Your mom is still sleeping. Stop the noise, please. (pause) Enough already!

Ida receives another text to herself:

MyKurtys says that he'll be over here in a few minutes. That's just enough time for Becky Lynn to finally tell you the secret that she came over here to tell you. Go on, Becky Lynn. Spill it, spill it, spill it!

Becky Lynn:

Hello? Excuse you? Don't just blurt out like that! I'll tell him when I'm ready to!

Ida:

Honesty? I'm surprised you haven't told him already. You tell him everything else and you've already told me. Why be so secretive? Don't be low-key now. Be "high-key."

Becky Lynn gestures toward herself and Zharquaviyont:

A & B. Alright? A & B.

Zharquaviyont:

Secretive about what?!

Ida:

Don't be on hush-mouth now. Either you tell him or I will.

Zharquaviyont:

Tell me what?!

Becky Lynn:

Now is not the time and this is not the place, Ida! You have to ease into something like that! *Common sense!*

> **Zharquaviyont's mother, LuPearl, returns from up-**
> **stairs. She's carrying some dishes that she rinses off**
> **and places into the dishwasher. After greeting the**
> **girls she addresses Zharquaviyont.**

LuPearl:

Hello, girls. (The girls wave to LuPearl.) Zharquaviyont?

Zharquaviyont:

Yes, ma'am.

LuPearl:

Your brother's plane just landed and I need you to drive me to the airport to pick him up.

Zharquaviyont:

Yes, ma'am.

LuPearl:

I'll be down in a minute. I just need to slip on my clothes.

Zharquaviyont:

Yes, ma'am. I'm ready whenever you are.

LuPearl exits the stage again via the stairway.

Ida whispers:
Come on. You're always talking about how "woke" you are. When are you gonna tell him? You should've told him already.

Becky Lynn:
Don't you have somewhere else you can be?

Ida:
Not at the moment, no. But MyKurtys is on his way over here. So… let's get to it.

Becky Lynn to Zharquaviyont:
Can you believe the nerve of this person? Some people just don't know when to butt out. (five-second pause) Anyway…Qua-Qua, give me your hand. I bought you something.

Zharquaviyont holds out his right hand. Becky Lynn takes hold of his left hand and places a ring on his ring finger.

Zharquaviyont:
Oooooh, girl. Is this for me? (pause) Becky Lynn, this is beautiful. And you know how I love me some jewelry.

Becky Lynn:
I know, right? (five-second pause) Do you like it?

Zharquaviyont:
Yes, I do! I love it! *This is straight fire.* (Zharquaviyont takes fifteen seconds to admire the jewelry, take a selfie and strikes a few poses.) *This is on fleek.* (pause) But no…I can't accept this.

Zharquaviyont begins to take the ring off.

Becky Lynn:
You're not gonna wear it?

Zharquaviyont:
This is a repeat...no. *This is very hard for me. You know how much I love me some jewelry.* **Zharquaviyont takes a deep breath and sighs.** But I'm not gonna be able to do it.

Becky Lynn:
Why not?

Zharquaviyont:
Because, honey, it looks way too expensive! That was very sweet of you but you shouldn't be spending your money on me. Here, take it back. (**Zharquaviyont hands the ring back to Becky Lynn and she receives it.**) You should be spending your money on more important things.

Becky Lynn:
But isn't you important, too?

Ida:
Aren't, Becky Lynn...aren't. The word is aren't! A-R-E-N-apostrophe T. Aren't you important, too?

Becky Lynn:
Butt out, Ida! If you say one more thing...I promise...*I swear to God!*

A car horn sounds from off stage.

Becky Lynn tilts her head from side to side while looking into Ida's face, waits for five seconds and says:
Well, bye! We all know that's for you. Please see yourself out.

The car horn sounds again from off stage.

Zharquaviyont:
Ida. He doesn't even have the common decency to knock on the door for you? Be for real.

Ida:
Gotta go. I'm about to make this play. Bye-bye.

Becky Lynn:
What is that thing people say when another person is about to leave when they should've already left? Something about the doorknob splitting them or something like that.

Ida makes that tooth-sucking sound, gives Qua-Qua a hug and says to Becky Lynn:
Pssst. Whatever. Take care of your flu-like symptoms.

Becky Lynn sarcastically:
Take care of your feminine hygiene.

Ida:
Speaking for yourself, I'm sure.

Ida exits the stage, snapping her fingers in Becky Lynn's face. Immediately after the door closes Becky Lynn speaks.

Becky Lynn:
Well...here it goes. Qua-Qua...Detroit left town and went back to Wahk'unna, you know, his second baby's momma. She's not the kind of female that would attract attention, where as I would. And at 5' 4", 105 pounds, you know she ain't got no booty. Anyway, he cheated on me with her but she cheated on him with some guy that just got out of rehab. And that makes me feel a *little* bit better.

Zharquaviyont:
Did I not tell you that would happen? Did I not tell you?

Becky Lynn:
You told me. All day I've been thinking that someone is after me. You know, to fight me or something like that. Does that make sense? I don't want or need anyone else's man. I think that I can find one of my own. Maybe I *should* get tested, though. Detroit wasn't worth my life.

Zharquaviyont:
Well, duh?! Other people may hate to say "I told you so" but I don't. *I told you so* or at least I tried to. You're always talking about common sense ain't all that common...is it? I tried to tell you not to move him into your momma's house to begin with. He was beneath you anyway.

Becky Lynn:
I know, right? He was childish in some ways and understood nothing.

But he *was* unique. I hate him...almost. But I won't soon forget him. How can I? Even after my mom kicked him out...he lived right down the street? My mom found out some disturbing news about him.

Zharquaviyont:
What news?

Becky Lynn:
He had been lying to her about how he was making his money.

Zharquaviyont:
So how was he making his money?

Becky Lynn:
He hustled himself up some fast-food uniforms and would leave the house every morning and be gone for hours, right? At the end of the week, he would bring her 300 dollars, right? Well, she came to find out that he was really out there slanging and that he was giving her drug money. So she put him out.

Zharquaviyont:
Was that your big secret?

Becky Lynn:
Noooooo! That's not it.

Zharquaviyont:
Then what is it? I've got to drive Momma to the airport to pick up my brother. *Spit it out!*

Becky Lynn takes a deep breath and says:

What I'm about to say could either go very well or very wrong. Does that make sense? I mean it could completely ruin our friendship. (pause) Okay? Here it goes. I'm like really nervous right now, okay? So don't interrupt me. What I'm about to say could possibly change the way we feel about each other and that would just kill me.

Zharquaviyont:

Becky Lynn, are you anywhere close to spitting it out?

Becky Lynn:

Okay. Here it goes. I've been having a lot of different thoughts of you in my mind lately. And those thoughts have had me feeling some kinda way. And…I've secretly had a crush on you for the last four years and I was wondering whether or not you felt the same way. And I'd like to take our relationship to the next level.

Zharquaviyont hangs his mouth open for two seconds.

Becky Lynn gestures to Zharquaviyont:

Qua-Qua, say something. Use your words.

Zharquaviyont:

I don't know what to say. Where is this coming from? What do you expect me to say after hearing something like that…all of a sudden like?

Becky Lynn:

Tell me that you feel the same way! Say you'll be my boyfriend!

Zharquaviyont:

Be your boyfriend? I can't!

Becky Lynn:

Why not?! (pause) Remember when I was going with Damadeus after we'd just moved here but it only lasted a quick, hot second? Everybody wants to be the first one to get the new girl, right? You know...that kind of thing. All he ever did was make me mad, cry and miserable. You were the one to help me move on. But I'm sure you don't want to hear all of the boring details.

Zharquaviyont:

That's right, Becky Lynn. Right now I don't have the time or patience for beating around the bush. You're all over the place with this conversation. If you're gonna tell me then tell me. If not...then don't. *I've got places to be and people who haven't seen me yet.* You're robbing me of my time. Either come with us to the airport or wave bye-bye!

Becky Lynn:

Wait, let me finish. I think that we should give a boyfriend/girlfriend relationship a try. You're my best friend in the world, we know everything about each other, we're together all the time, we complete each other's sentences, we have an awesome connection and...

Zharquaviyont:

Becky Lynn, you already know that I'm gay!!! Where is this coming from?

Becky Lynn pauses for three seconds and says:

Excuse me? I thought you were bi?

Zharquaviyont:

I'm gay, Becky Lynn…just gay. I like guys and only guys. But I'm flattered, though, *I think*, that you would think of me that way.

Becky Lynn:

Flattered?! You're flattered? Are you trying to be funny with me right now? Because if you are, you're being very cruel and hurtful. I thought that you were bi. I've seen you kissing other girls, girls other than me!

Zharquaviyont:

Platonic relationships, Becky Lynn! They were friend-girls, not girl-friends! There's a difference! I kiss them *and you* because I lose my Chapstick and I need lip gloss. I'm not bisexual! I'm only attracted to guys! *Everybody knows that!*

Zharquaviyont and Becky Lynn both pause for three seconds.

Zharquaviyont:

Well, this is an awkward moment. Use your words, Becky Lynn.

Becky Lynn:

Are you making fun of me?!

Zharquaviyont smiles with his hand over his mouth like a girl would:

No. I'm not.

Becky Lynn:

I've never been so humiliated. How could you do this to me?! You're gay?! We're best friends! Why didn't you ever tell me that you liked guys exclusively?! (pause) Stop laughing at me!

Zharquaviyont whispers:
Keep your voice down. (pause) We're best friends. How could you not know that I liked guys exclusively?! And don't yell at me. I'm not making a fool of you. You're making a fool of yourself!

Becky Lynn attempts to leave and Zharquaviyont grabs her arm.

Zharquaviyont:
I'm sorry. I wasn't trying to hurt you. I don't know what else to say. Please don't go. Not like this.

Becky Lynn slaps his hand away and says:
Don't touch me, A-cup! Who knows where your hands have been?! I should've known that the sugar in your tank didn't swing both ways, "sweet boy."

Zharquaviyont:
Calm down, Becky Lynn…you seem very thirsty all of a sudden. I mean…I'm shook. I don't know where this is coming from, but honey, you're doing too much and at the wrong tree.

> **Becky Lynn leaves the scene. Ten seconds pass before LuPearl enters after Becky Lynn closes the door behind her in order to transition from Scene 1 into Scene 2.**

Scene 2-Introduction of Franklin

LuPearl returns from upstairs, takes the keys from her purse and hands them to Zharquaviyont as she says:
Do I even want to know what all that was about?

As LuPearl takes more dishes to the kitchen, Zharquaviyont shoves the keys into his pocket as he says:
No, ma'am. It was nothing, Momma, just some unnecessary drama. Are you ready to go?

LuPearl:
Where teenaged girls are concerned, you should expect some drama…most of it's unnecessary. I try to tell you and your brothers, all the time, about conniving little narrow-butt girls. Nothing *but* trouble. I know. I too was once a conniving little narrow-butt girl. (pause) Carry my purse out to the truck for me, baby. I'm ready.

> **When Zharquaviyont approaches and opens the door, his brother, Franklin walks through.**

Franklin:
Surprise!!!! Hey, Momma!!!!

LuPearl hugs her son and is almost in tears.

LuPearl, almost out of breath:
Boy?! What am I gonna do with you? How did you get here so fast? You just called from the airport.

Franklin hugs LuPearl again and says:
My plane landed three and a half hours ago, Momma. I had to give myself enough time to catch a cab and surprise you. Momma! I'm so glad to see and hug my Momma! I love you, Momma.

LuPearl
Not as much as I love you, baby. Not as much as I love you. Boy, you're something else. Say hello to your brother.

Franklin examines his brother's "outfit" and pauses for two seconds:
Zharquaviyont.

Zharquaviyont:
Franklin.

After a short and awkward pause of two more seconds, Franklin says:
What's up, "Fam"?! Same old fits, huh? I see you're still wearing those pastel colors and pants with no pockets on the back.

Zharquaviyont:
Uhn-uhn. Uhn-uhn. Don't come for me…'cause I'll cut you up.

Franklin:
Can't you find somebody to help you with your wardrobe?

Zharquaviyont:
Please…everything about me is "on fleek" *and you already know.* (pause) I see you're still ugly! I can change my clothes but you're gonna need a plastic surgeon. Boo-ya!

Franklin:
Okay…okay. Good one…good one. Give your brother a hug, small-fry.

Zharquaviyont stops Franklin in his tracks and says:
Don't be callin' me small-fry. I had more than enough *of that* when we were kids. A hug won't be necessary. No need to overdo it. An almost kiss on the cheek will more than suffice.

Franklin:
A what?! An almost kiss on the cheek?! Forget that. How about a handshake between two men, small-fry?

Zharquaviyont holds out his hand in a feminine manner and says:
Fine.

The two brothers shake each other's hands after Franklin demonstrates just how to execute a proper masculine handshake.

Zharquaviyont:

So…how have you been? (pause) Have there been any wild parties or anything exciting going on up there? I know that you've been getting into everything.

Franklin:

I don't act like that anymore, little man. I'm doing very well. Thanks for asking. I've actually just been trying to stay out of "woman trouble." **Franklin pounds his chest.** Right now…I'm just trying to keep things cool inside of here.

Zharquaviyont:

Okay. Look at me closely. Don't you recognize me?

"Qua-Qua" frames his own face and says:

It's me… Zharquaviyont…your brother? *I know you.* You can't tell me just anything. *I know when you're lying.*

Franklin:

No, little brother. You're thinking about the old Franklin. This is the new Franklin. I don't act like that anymore. Whether you believe it or not…is your issue…in your Capri pants.

Franklin suddenly puts Zharquaviyont into an unexpected and unappreciated bear hug.

LuPearl:

Awwwww. Now that's a picture. Let me get my camera. Oh…just wait one minute.

LuPearl opens the front door and takes a look outside. Her sons release each other.

Franklin:

Momma, what in the world are you doing?

LuPearl:

I'm checking for your latest girlfriend. (pause) Who is it this time? I know you've got one. Where is she? Last I heard it was some girl named Ashan'e. But if it's that Bethany...child, she can't even set foot in my house. I don't even want *her in my yard.* You need to take her right on away from here right now.

Franklin:

Momma, I'm happy to say...that Bethany and I are no longer together. And Ashan'e and I agreed to see other people. I'm single now and hope to keep it that way for a while. Both of the breakups were pretty ugly.

Zharquaviyont:

They both caught you with other girls, didn't they?

Franklin takes a deep breath, sighs and hangs his head:

Franklin:

Yes.

LuPearl:

What was that pretty little Hispanic girl's name, Franklin?

Franklin:

What Hispanic girl, Momma?

LuPearl:

The little quiet one that you brought with you that weekend that didn't say much.

Franklin:

Oh…you mean Mirica. She just wasn't very confident with her English, Momma. That's all.

LuPearl:

Well, anyway…you let the good one get away. You may as well hang it up now. (pause) See…I know what happened. I thought highly of her and her parents thought highly of you. So there was no way that was gonna work out. (pause) Had I not liked her and her folks not liked you…she'd be right here or you'd be right there with them at the dinner table.

Franklin:

Momma, when? When…when…when are you going to stop bringing up Linda?! She got away, Momma. Sometimes…you've got to own up to the fact that you messed up your relationship. I've done that…and moved on with my life.

LuPearl:

Of all the girls you've ever brought here…she was top shelf. She was a sweet girl…perfect for you in every way. She was kindhearted, sang solo in the church choir, a straight-A student with a clear plan for her life and a multiple beauty pageant winner. She was a very distinguished young woman with a smile that would force a person to put on some sunglasses. She was a little chocolate doll.

Franklin:

Believe me, Momma. *I remember all of that!* 35-29-44! All…of…that. Barrel racer…she loved horses. But seriously, Momma, the thing I miss most about Linda…the conversations. And whenever we hadn't seen each other for a few days…she'd hug me and say, "Ahhhhh, back where I belong." (pause) Last I heard, though, she was someone's wife. After a while, I called her, Mom…and she told me that Linda had gotten out of the Air Force, gotten married, left the Philippines and moved back home to Rayville, Louisiana. Living in the past isn't good for anyone, Momma. And that's just what Linda represents…the past. Let it go, Momma…I have.

Zharquaviyont:

As usual…both of you have the girlfriends mixed up. Linda wasn't shaped up like that. You're describing Dewberry. Dewberry was thick. *That's* who *you're* describing. She was a sweet girl but Linda could use about four more pounds of booty.

LuPearl:

Zharquaviyont!

Zharquaviyont:

I'm just trying to set the record straight, Momma…that's all. It was Lynn that rode the horses, Anell sang in the choir, Maude Esther was the straight-A student and little Carol was the "light-skinned" one with the pretty smile. Remember? She ran track. One girl couldn't have had all of those qualities. And remember Kelly Fitzgerald? She and Momma were the exact same size.

LuPearl:

You don't know what size I am, boy. Carol wasn't "light-skinned." She was "paper-sack brown." And Lynn didn't ride horses. It was little Gigi who loved the horses. Lynn was in Vet School.

Franklin:

Yeah…Dewberry! That's right. It *was* Dewberry. 35-29-44! She wasn't too fine…she was three fine, borderline four fine! *How do you remember all of those different girls' names?*

Zharquaviyont:

Like I said…I know you…been here for all of it. And the truth ain't in ya! Nowhere!

LuPearl:

Well…anyway, if you've really moved on…then that's a good thing. But to me she'll always be the daughter-in-law that I should've had. Every April 19, I buy her one of those cute little Aries necklace/earring sets that she liked so much, just in case she ever happens to stop by. And I send a birthday card to her mother's house.

Franklin, clapping his hands once:

If you want to do that, Momma, then do it. She's not…coming…by. And apparently…you're sending the birthday card to the wrong house. Do they ever come back "Return to Sender"?

LuPearl:

No. Not even one. But what if I told you that she called me the other night to offer her condolences for your father's passing?

Zharquaviyont:

Which one, Momma? Please tell me that you knew who you were speaking with over the phone.

LuPearl:

She told me who she was. I knew exactly who I was speaking with.

Franklin:

It makes no difference who she was speaking with because I'm no longer involved with them. Why are we even talking about this? Momma…let it go…please. She's not coming back. And neither are Regina, Anell, Lynn, Maude Esther, Carol or Mona Marie Mason…especially not Mona Marie Mason. Aren't you gonna say anything about the car, Momma? I know you saw it.

LuPearl:

You know your Momma, don't you? You know that I'm gonna ask you about that car. Whose Jag is that? And I know that you're trying to change the subject, too. You're not as slick as you think.

Franklin chuckles and says:

It belongs to the father of one of my friends from school. Her name is Shevi and her parents live about fifty miles from here. We flew in together and took a cab to her parents' house. It's Shevi's car but it's in her father's name. She let me drive it up here for the funeral. She's not my girlfriend. She is just a friend for R.O.T.C., Momma. That's all.

LuPearl:

Boy! Do you know what's going on out there on the highways all across this country? If you get pulled over for drivin' a fancy car like that, you could lose your life. Drivin' while you're black is dangerous.

Zharquaviyont:
That's right, Momma. You tell him.

LuPearl:
You give that car back to that girl and ride home with us like you're supposed to. You don't need to be driving other folks' cars, especially other folks' parents' cars. Don't do that again! Do you hear me?

Franklin:
Yes, ma'am. I'll stay out of other people's fancy cars. I won't do it again…I promise. Alright?

Zharquaviyont:
Wait a minute. Wait a minute. What I want to know is…who was it this time, Franklin, the roommate, squad leader, her sister, her mother? Who did Bethany and Ashane catch you with?

Franklin:
Well, if you must know, Messy-Wesley of the paparazzi…it was with Bethany's roommate on parents' weekend but that's not the point. I've given myself a fresh start, Momma. I'm considering myself a re-committed virgin. No more foolishness until marriage. I'm done with that.

LuPearl:
My baby! I know that's right! *You'd better get some fat on your head!*

Zharquaviyont:

Momma…*you know you don't believe that.* A pair of lips will say anything. It's getting *real deep in here!*

Zharquaviyont puts his earbuds into his ears in order to escape into his music.

LuPearl:

Zharquaviyont, now don't start. Your brother hadn't been here but five minutes. Behave, both of you. Take them thangs outta your ears when I'm talking to you, boy!

Franklin:

Momma, it's okay. He's just playing.

LuPearl:

Boy…are they starving you up there? You look like you've lost a lot of weight! Come on over here, sit down and let your Momma fix you a plate.

Zharquaviyont:

He's almost twenty-three years old now, Momma. He can fix his own plate. Next thing you'll be callin' him "sugar-booger."

Franklin:

Momma…you know I'd love that! But I saw Aunt Rosie at the corner and she wants me to come over there. She said that everybody's gonna be there and that she's been calling on you all week. She wanted you to let her know when you were going to the funeral home.

Zharquaviyont:

Really, Franklin? You've been here not even five minutes and you're already putting yo daddy's people ahead of Momma?! That's really savage.

Franklin to LuPearl:

Momma, it's not like that. I'm only gonna be here this week. I don't want anybody to say that I didn't come by to see them. But if you don't want me to go, then I won't go.

Zharquaviyont:

That's what you shoulda said in the first place. Oooooh! You make me sick! I can't stand you!

LuPearl to Zharquaviyont:

No, son. That's a very mature attitude to have. (Then to Franklin) You used to say, "If anybody wants to see me…they can come out to my momma's house." (pause) But this is a time when family should come together and console each other. Franklin, you go on ahead and be with yur father's people. I'll see you when you get back.

Zharquaviyont:

Momma!

Franklin:

Thank you, Momma. Knowing my cousins, they're probably gonna be playing some football.

LuPearl nods, faces Zharquaviyont, puts her index finger to her lips and whispers:

Shhhh.

They then hug each other for three seconds.

Zharquaviyont:

Momma, this ain't right. But fine…fine, fine, fine.

LuPearl:

Zharquaviyont, don't be that way. That's ugly.

Zharquaviyont:

Yes, ma'am. If you like it…I love it. (repeat)

LuPearl:

Zharquaviyont…

Zharquaviyont looks directly at Franklin and says:

Momma…you know we're gonna need a lot more food and supplies in this house now that "ya son" is here. He eats just to see how much he *can* eat. That greedy thang will eat us out of house and home.

LuPearl:

Ain't that the truth! Franklin…Zharquaviyont and I will probably still be at the grocery store by the time you get back home. Do you have your house key to be able to let yourself back in?

Franklin:

Yes, ma'am, I have it. Momma, I'm gonna prepare an outstanding pancake breakfast for us in the morning. I plan to sleep in a little bit so breakfast won't be ready until 0730. I'll see you guys a little bit later, alright?

**Franklin hugs and kisses his mother again and at-
tempts to hug Zharquaviyont. He refuses. Franklin
exits through the front door. Zharquaviyont's cell-
phone rings and he answers. It's his other brother,
Donovan, on the line.**

Zharquaviyont:

Hey, Donavan (pause), same soup different day (pause). What's up on
your end? (pause) You know your brother, "Mr. Popularity," just got
here, right? (pause) Well, he was here five minutes before he ran out
the door to be with his father's people....completely shunning my
Momma's feelings.

LuPearl:

Zharquaviyont, stop that. Give me that phone.

Zharquaviyont:

Donovan...Momma wants to speak to you.

LuPearl:

Donovan Darius Hampton Jr., where are you? (pause) Are you gonna
get to make it, baby? (pause) Uh-hunh. (pause) Uh-hunh. I see. Do you
want to tell him or do you want me to do it? (pause) Uh-hunh. I
thought as much. He went over to his Aunt Rosie's. (pause) No, Donovan, I don't need you to send me any money. I told you to cancel my
allotment and that's what I meant.

Zharquaviyont:

Tell him that he can sure send me some.

LuPearl:

You just make sure you're payin' that child support on time. That's what you do! (pause) You're laughin' but I'm serious. Having two women pregnant at the same time was cool at first but it's not cool now, is it? Uh-hunh, not as much as I love you, baby. Zharquaviyont said bye. Okay. Immm, bye-bye.

LuPearl ends the call and appears to be a little upset.

Zharquaviyont:

Momma, are you okay?

LuPearl puts on a brave face and says:

Momma's alright, baby. Everything is *alright*. Come on over here and help me make out a grocery list. I should've already done it but with everything happening, well, I just forgot.

The telephone rings and LuPearl answers. Zharquaviyont eavesdrops on the conversation.

LuPearl:

Hello. (pause) No, Franklin's not here right now. He just stepped out. May I ask who's calling? (pause) Stacy? Oh. (pause) Yes, I am his mother. (pause) Well, I hope that he had some nice things to say about me. (pause) Oh, you're his tutor? Well, why does he need a tutor? He makes all A's. (pause) Oh, I see. (pause) Well, Stacy…I'll tell him that you called as soon as he gets back, alright? (pause) Yes…it was nice speaking with you as well. (pause) Immm bye-bye.

Zharquaviyont:

Who was that, Momma?

LuPearl:

It was some young lady calling for Franklin. She said that she was tutoring him in Korean.

Zharquaviyont:

Korean?! (pause) Immm hmmm. Well, whatever. (pause) *He's never needed a tutor before.* What changed? (dramatic pause) Are you gonna sing at the funeral tomorrow, Momma?

LuPearl:

No, I'm just gonna pay my respects and keep my seat. I'm sure that they have way more speakers and singers than they need. The first time someone gets out of line...I'm going to respectfully remove myself from the services.

Zharquaviyont:

Surely there won't be any clowning at the funeral, Momma...the one place where there should be some decorum. He left you in charge of his final arrangements even though you had been divorced for years. He put it in black and white, so what is the dispute?

LuPearl:

Decorum?! There is a chance that there could be some clowning. Arguing about who's gonna ride in the limo, excessive theatrics, personal expressions, people asking for money, stopping the funeral procession for bathroom breaks and snacks and violence could break out at any moment. Honey....I know these people.

Zharquaviyont:

The only reason that they're treating you this way is that they thought that they'd get some money on the back end of his death. He left an inheritance for Franklin and he didn't leave them a *dime*. Hopefully blood won't be spilled at the church or the cemetery, Momma.

LuPearl:

There was nothing to leave! And that was the way he intended. He left a substantial amount of money behind for your brother. He wanted to be buried in his uniform, in the bronze casket with the high-gloss gold mirrored exterior, a purple velvet-lined interior, nine dozen purple roses and a heart level tandem mausoleum crypt. And he wanted all of the attendees to have an engraved golf ball with an eagle about his name and "B.R.U.H.Z." on the other side. His sisters especially felt that that was wasteful spending.

Zharquaviyont:

Even though it was in his will in black and white?! He made you the executor of his will and that's all there is to it. They'll just have to accept it. Ain't nobody gonna be trippin' with my Momma, right in front of my face. I put that on everything I love.

LuPearl:

Well...I'm telling you right now that all of the above is possible. When I make my move to leave, I need you to be right on my hip. After the 21-gun salute, they're gonna present me with his flag. That's when we're leaving. I don't have the patience for that fake weeping and wailing.

Zharquaviyont:

Well, I'm telling *you*, that I for one am very proud of how you could put your differences aside with his sisters and put together a fine funeral service for Colonel Potts. Because of you, he'll have all of the finest things that that funeral home had. He'll be laid to rest in the same way that he lived…with the highest level of dignity.

LuPearl:

He was a fine man. Franklin Ali Solomon Potts II never hurt anyone. It was the least that I could do to endure the silliness of his sisters. But I thank you for the compliment.

Zharquaviyont:

You're welcome, Momma. But tell me something…if the Colonel never remarried, why do you think he purchased a tandem mausoleum crypt? What is a tandem mausoleum crypt?

LuPearl:

Don't be coy with me, boy. You know what it is and you know why. He wanted me to be laid to rest with him. Whichever one of us passed away first would be entombed feet first. The other would be entombed head first…for all eternity…yet another thing that his sisters didn't care for.

Zharquaviyont:

That's beautiful, Momma.

LuPearl:

Yes, it was. (pause) Yes, it was. And while it's on my mind…I want to talk to you boys about my own pre-need funeral arrangements. I haven't arranged anything at all. And until I got involved with the Colonel's arrangements, I had no idea of what all was involved or what it would cost. So what I want to do is

Zharquaviyont:

Naaaah, Momma. I don't wanna talk about that. You're perfectly healthy.

LuPearl:

I'm not talking about right this minute. But we do need to talk about this. Maybe not today but we, along with both of your knucklehead brothers, *will* talk about this. Ya Momma ain't no spring chicken.

Zharquaviyont:

You're as young as you feel....right, Momma?

LuPearl:

And I feel that the time has come for me to discuss this with my children. I'm gonna have everything all written out...line by line. They gave me this thing called a pre-planning guide. And I want you to record me speaking to the audience. I'm considering a cremation ceremony.

Zharquaviyont:

Well, back to the matter at hand, Momma. I've already made out the grocery list. All you have to do is say yes or no. That way, we won't have to go up and down each aisle or end up with a lot of unnecessary things. They call that "impulse buying."

LuPearl:

Okay? Look at my baby, taking care of his Momma. We're probably gonna be waist deep in fried chicken, chicken spaghetti and chicken pot pie, but let's go down the list anyway. (pause) Zharquaviyont...don't you ever leave your Momma. I don't know what I'd ever do without you here takin care of me. I love you, baby.

Zharquaviyont:
Not as much as I love you, Momma. (pause) Now before we forget... we need to make sure we go by and pick up you're prescription from Dr. Etter's pharmacy.

> **Zharquaviyont sits down, crossed his legs, takes out a list and a pen and begins to go down the list of items. LuPearl says either yes or no to the items as they are being read aloud. The telephone rings but they both ignore it.**

Shopping list

Mac & Cheese
3 large cans of tuna
Lotion
Laundry detergent
2 dozen Lrg. Brown eggs
Lrg. Pork maple Sausage

Gallon of orange juice
Butterfly shrimp
Gallon of apple juice
1 package of Gravy mix
5 T-bone steaks
Steak Sauce

Fresh fruit medley
1 bag of Flour
Fresh garlic cloves
Ketchup
Catfish fillets
Collard greens

LuPearl

Baby, listen…we don't have to go over the entire list right now. We're wasting time that way; we can go over the rest of the list in the truck on the way. But *you've done a good job, though*, putting the list together. Come on…let's go so that we can get on back and get the food on.

Zharquaviyont:

Yes, ma'am. Sounds like we're goin shoppin'! (pause) Let me have the keys, Momma…I'll go out and warm up the truck.

LuPearl:

The keys are in my purse, aren't they? Wait a minute. Didn't I already hand you the keys?

Zharquaviyont:

No, ma'am. I don't think so.

LuPearl:

Are you sure? I could've sworn that I handed you those keys.

Zharquaviyont checks his pockets and laughs before saying:

I'm sorry, Momma. I had the keys in my pocket the whole time. I'm trippin'.

With hands on her hips, LuPearl shoots him a Momma's look and says:

See there. That's exactly what I mean. You and your brothers don't listen worth a quarter. I've always tried to tell you and your brothers to watch. W.A.T.C.H. Do you remember what each letter stands for, Zharquaviyont?

Zharquaviyont, speaking with his hands on his hips just like his mother:

Yes, Momma…I remember. Do we really have to go through this now?

LuPearl:

Did I ask you about it now? Don't get smart with *me*, boy. I'm not one of your little friends. You'd better watch your tone with me. (pause) Now let's hear it. What does "W" stand for?

Zharquaviyont reluctantly says:

<u>W</u> is for ways. We need to always watch the way we do things. <u>A</u> is for attitude. A negative attitude can destroy anything. <u>T</u> is for tongue. We must always be careful about what and how we say things. <u>C</u> is for company. We must always watch the company we keep and the people that we associate with.

LuPearl was a 6-feet-1-inch-tall, 190-pound self-assured woman who didn't play:

Lose the attitude, boy! Didn't you just tell me that you're supposed to watch your bad attitude?!

Zharquaviyont:

Whaaaaaat? What'd I say?

LuPearl:

What does the "H" stand for?

Zharquaviyont speaking simultaneously:

What'd I do?

LuPearl:

You know what you're doing! What does the "H" in "WATCH" stand for?

Zharquaviyont:

<u>H</u> stands for hands and feet. We can keep ourselves out of a world of trouble if we control our hands and feet.

LuPearl:

Immm hmmm. I guess.

Scene 3-Introduction of Becky Lynn's mother, Paula

There is a knock at the door and Zharquaviyont answers it. Paula enters the scene, looking all around the room.

Paula:

Hey, LuPearl, how you doing, girl? You sure are holding your weight. You're taking good care of that girlish figure. (pause) Tell me something, though…who is driving that Jag-wagon in your driveway?

LuPearl:

Hello, Paula. I'm on my way out to the grocery store. I don't have time for this right now. What can I do for you? What is it that you need?

Paula:

Girl, I just came over here to see who was driving that Jag-wagon! I drove around the block three times just to see who was gonna come out and get into the car. And when nobody came out, I called. When you didn't answer, I figured I'd just come over here. I said to myself that it might be somebody in here that I needed to come and see!

LuPearl:

Paula...you're way too nosey to still be livin'. I don't have *time* for this right now. I just told you that I'm on my way out to the store. Now turn around and hit the door. Come on, heifer...I've got things to do! Hit the door...hit the door.

Paula doesn't bulge:

Now don't act like that, LuPearl. Tell me who is drivin' that fancy car. At least tell me that.

LuPearl:

Paula, that ain't none of your business...and you know it. Now you're trying my patience on purpose and I know it. Before I lose my patience, you should probably get to steppin'.

Paul takes a seat:

Well, fine. Keep your little secret. What I really came to talk to you about was the day I had at the welfare office earlier today. You remember me talkin' about "Rude Gertrude," right? Well, she's worse now that she's the little assistant to the office manager. My old pastor always used to say, "If you ever want to find out who a person really is...give them *just a little bit of authority* and a set of keys. That's all that it'll take." *That's all that it'll take!* Oh, and my daughters? I don't know what to do with them so I just take them up there to the pastor. They act like two entirely different people!

LuPearl:

That's because they are two entirely different people. Let me tell you something.

66

Zharquaviyont:

Momma?

LuPearl:

Not now, baby, I'm talkin'. Paula…I've loved my children equally but differently.

Paula:

What do you mean? I don't understand.

LuPearl:

Even identical twins are their own people. And your younger daughter is just trying to see where she fits into the picture. You have to treat them all as individuals. All three of my boys have to be handled differently. I'm just giving you my quick take of the situation…take it or leave it.

Zharquaviyont exits the scene.

LuPearl:

My oldest boy, Donovan…he just needs some gentle persuasion from time to time. He usually does what I tell him to do. Now my middle son…he needs a kick to his back pockets from time to time when he gets too full of himself. But that one that just walked out here? That's my heart. He's had more heartache than you can imagine. Paula…his ten-year-old half-sister, Dion, was at home sleeping in her bed and was shot and killed by gang violence in the street.

Paula:

Oh, my God. LuPearl, I'm so sorry. I didn't know that. I did not know that.

LuPearl:

At her funeral, his father was so grief-stricken that when her casket was lowered he jumped down into her grave and took his own life. There was also a time when I was working two jobs and I had to leave him with my sister. The other two were involved in activities at school but Zharquaviyont was only six. I found out that my own sister had been molesting my baby. To this day he tells me, "Momma, no matter how many times I wash, I can never get her smell off of my hands." So you see, Paula, your girls have to be handled differently because they are different.

Paula:

LuPearl, I'm so, so sorry. I didn't mean to bring up such a painful memory. I'm feeling very small right now. Did you ever seek any professional help for him? And whatever happened with your sister?

LuPearl approaches the door as she is speaking:

Now Paula…you're about to force me to be rude like Gertrude. I've already told you that I was on my way out. So…

> **As LuPearl opens the door Franklin reenters the scene wearing a tight, white and soaking-wet t-shirt. Fifteen seconds later Zharquaviyont reenters the scene.**

Paula:

Oh, my. Well, now…who is this? You've gotten your t-shirt *all wet.*

LuPearl:

Paula, this is my middle son, Franklin. I call him sugar-booger. He goes to military college in another state. He's gonna be a Second Lieutenant in the United States Military when he graduates. Just like his father. He's just here for his father's funeral. Isn't he handsome?

Franklin extends his hand to Paula:
Hello, ma'am. How are you?

Paula:
Oh, my. *Very nice.* Girl, he is handsome. How old are you, Franklin?

Franklin:
On January 28, I'll be twenty-three, ma'am.

Paula:
Girl, that's just the right age to be in life. If I was younger, I'd give him a run for his money.

LuPearl:
What?! Excuse me?

Paula:
I'm just joking, LuPearl. Don't take everything so seriously.

LuPearl:
Watch yourself. Alright?! Watch yourself. You're talking to and about my child. He'll be going back to his campus in a couple of days. He's the one drivin' the Jag. Now goodbye to you!

Paula:
Well, you don't have to be so rude, LuPearl. I was just asking. (pause)

Well, anyhoo, it was nice to meet you, young man. Maybe we can sit down and visit a little while before you go back to school. What school do you go to?

LuPearl:

Now Paula, I know…that you didn't just stand here, in my doorway, and throw yourself at my son a second time, right here in front of me… and you have the audacity to call me rude? Don't make me lose my religion. I've worked to hard to get to this point in my life.

Paula:

Calm down, LuPearl. Don't get your blood pressure all up. I'll just let myself out. (pause) Call me later. (pause) It was very nice meeting you, Franklin.

Paula exits the scene with a little wave and some assistance from LuPearl.

Zharquaviyont:

I thought that you were gonna have to put your hands on her to get her to leave, Momma. But anyway…that was some quick football, Franklin.

Franklin:

Mind *your* business, small-fry. Grown folks are talking.

LuPearl:

Franklin, you received a call from a young lady while you were out. She said that her name was Stacy and that she was your Korean tutor? Why do you need a Korean tutor?

Franklin:

No. She's not my Korean tutor. She's Korean and we're in R.O.T.C. together.

Zharquaviyont:

Don't you have any male friends in R.O.T.C.? Sounds to me like R.O.T.C. has far too many females in it. That's your problem. That's what's wrong with you.

Franklin:

Anyway...Momma, I'm going to be taking a Korean language class next semester and she's helping me to get ahead of the class. I'll hit her up later. Look, she gave me this coin to carry around with me to remind me to keep practicing Korean.

> **Franklin pulls a Korean 100 won from his pocket
> in order to show to his mother.**

LuPearl:

Well, that's good, baby, but why do you need to learn Korean?

Franklin:

Well, I have a suspicion that after my graduation...my first duty assignment will be in Korea. So it would behoove me to have a firm grip on the language prior to.

Zharquaviyont:

Do you really believe that Momma is gonna fall for this BS? She knows good and well that you're not studying any *Korean!* You're studying

Korean Stacy. That's what he's doing, Momma. If you're supposedly learning Korean…let's hear some then.

Franklin:
Well, as I stated previously…I'm new to the language with no formal instruction…right? But "Cho Un Achim" means "Good morning." "Cho Un Ohu" means "Good afternoon." "Koma wa yo" is a way to say "Thank you." "Chun Man He Yo" is "You're welcome." "Ahn yan seyo" is "Hello" or "Good morning." "Gom Som Ni Da" is another way of saying "Thank you." "Bahn Ga Wah yo" is how you would say "Good to see you again." When leaving from a room of other people you would say "Ahn Yiga Se Yo." So as you can see, Stacy's already taught me a great deal.

Zharquaviyont:
How do we know that that's not all bunch gibberish? You're the absolute very best liar that I personally have ever seen. *And I'd just bet she's taught you a great deal.*

Franklin does three chopping motions to his throat in Zharquaviyont's direction.

Franklin:
Hey, hey, hey. Stacy is a very nice girl. Don't make accusations about her like that. You don't know her. Momma, I'm gonna take a shower and change before the barbecue at 1600. Are you guys on your way out?

LuPearl:
Yeah, baby. We've got to get to the grocery store and on back so that I can get the food on. We'll be back in a little while. Are you hungry now?

Franklin:

Yes, ma'am. I'll probably just have a little light snack after my shower but still be ready to chow down at the barbecue. I know that Uncle Charles is gonna throw down on the pit *today!*

LuPearl:

Well, let me fix you a little something before I go out.

Zharquaviyont:

Momma, that's a grown man! Let "sugar booger" fix his own snack! *He ain't no baby!*

Franklin says with a sarcastic chuckle:

That's right, Sweet-Boy. I'm a man. (pause) You know, I've always wondered something. Why is it that the hairstylist always has the worst hairstyle? Your hair is always jacked up. Why is that? (repeat twice)

> **Zharquaviyont steps toward Franklin in anger. Lu-Pearl steps in between them.**

LuPearl:

Zharquaviyont…go on out to the truck. Go-to-the-truck! Let me have a word alone with your brother. Go on now! Here, take my purse.

Franklin:

Qua-Qua? I'm gonna say this before you go. (repeat) If my comment upset you…I'm sorry. But look at it this way. I've said far worse…and you know it.

Zharquaviyont swings his mother's purse over his left shoulder the same way that his mother does and exits the scene with a finger snap in a circular motion.

LuPearl:

Now Franklin, you shouldn't torment him like that. You know he's a sensitive child. He's just having an identity crisis right now due to childhood trauma. You know what happened to him.

Franklin:

I didn't mean anything by it, Momma. That's just how three brothers grow up talking to each other.

LuPearl:

He needs our love and support, not jokes and ridicule. He has internal turmoil. He's probably out there in the truck crying right now. He thinks that you're always outdoing him.

Franklin:

I am outdoing him! Momma I'm up by four, out by five and in by six every day. Momma, I work my tail off to be where I am…like a man! If he stays on the path he's on, he'll be forty years old and still living under your roof. If he's gonna be gay. Fine! Gay people have careers too, Momma! Every tub has to sit on its own bottom. The time has come for him to grow up, Momma. And you have to let him be your son, not your daughter.

LuPearl:

He thinks that you hate him! You need to tell your brother that you love him, unconditionally, before you leave here and go back to that military college world that you think everybody should live it!

Franklin:

I don't hate him, Momma. He's my little brother and I'll always love him, no matter what. But he's not one of your girlfriends, Momma!

LuPearl:

Why are you standing here tellin' me that?! You know what? (pause) Maybe I didn't use the language that we use to use. **LuPearl approaches Franklin.** I'm not askin' you. I'm tellin' you. You're gonna tell your brother that you love him or suffer physical consequences! Do you hear me talking to you, Negro?!!!

Franklin instinctively snaps to attention:

Ma'am, yes, ma'am!

> **LuPearl exits without another word, slamming the door behind her for dramatic effect. Ten seconds pass before the sound of a vehicle driving away is heard from off stage.**

Scene 4-Franklin Meets Becky Lynn and Ida

Franklin looks skyward and says:
My family. Myyyyyyy family. Why would I be shown the light while my people are left in the dark? (pause) Why do I keep coming back here?! (pause) There is nothing but pain here for me!

> **Franklin begins to pace back and forth. He removes his t-shirt, drops to the floor and begins doing diamond-styled pushups. He counts out twenty-five. Suddenly the doorbell rings and Franklin stands to answer the door. It's Becky Lynn and Ida.**

Franklin:
Yes? Is there something that I can do for you?

Becky Lynn takes a moment to collect herself and says:
OMG. Uhhh, hello. Ummm…uhhh…oh my God. (pause) Is Zharquaviyont available? We'd really like to speak with him, if possible. (pause) Is Zharquaviyont here by any chance?

Franklin reaches for his shirt and attempts to cover himself:
No, he's not. He and my mother went out to the grocery store. Hold on, let me guess. You're Becky Lynn and Ida, right? The squad?

Becky Lynn:
Yes! That's right! I'm Becky Lynn and she has a boyfriend. Today is her birthday so big whoopty-doo…right? Every day is somebody's birthday, right? (pause) Are you Zharquaviyont's brother Franklin? You guys don't look anything alike!

Ida unintentionally drops her phone. As she bends down to retrieve it, she places her right hand behind her back in order to prevent the possibility of exposing herself. This is a very classy, self-respecting, dignified and ladylike thing to do. Franklin witnesses this act and is very impressed with Ida. And so…he "sends the sharks out" (flirting).

Franklin:
Yes. I'm the middle brother. Same mother…different fathers.

Becky Lynn:
Zharquaviyont told us that it's been a whole minute since you've been back. So welcome home.

Franklin smoothly reaches past Becky Lynn and extends his hand in introduction to Ida. He raises and lowers his head in a slow and seductive manner as Ida raises her hand, almost in a trancelike state, to shake his. Ida smiles, takes his hand, nods her head and says:
"Immm hmmm."

Franklin:

Potts, Franklin Ali Solomon III. Ida…right? Tienes una sonrise my bonita. (You have a pretty smile.) Sabes que la sequnda mejor cosa que peudes hacer con tus labios. (You know, it's the second-best thing that you can do with your lips.)

Ida:

I speak English too, man!

Franklin:

Buenas tardes, Ida. (Good afternoon, Ida.) Se que una joven atractiva como tu se cansa de que los chicos flirteen con ella. La mayoria de las veces ella simplemente no quiere ser molestada. ¿Estoy en lo correcto o incorrecto? (I know that an attractive young lady such as yourself gets so tired of guys flirting with her. Most times she just doesn't want to be bothered. Am I right or wrong?)

Ida:

Por la tarde, si tienesrazon, pero como supiste y como esta? (Afternoon, yes, you are so right but how did you know and how are you?)

Franklin:

Bien, gracias. ¿Y usted? (Fine, thank you. And you?)

Ida:

Muy bien, gracias. (Very well, thanks.)

Franklin:

Me gusta su camiseta de futbol Colin Kapernick. Eso es lo que pasa.

Mucho gusto, Ida. (I like your Colin Kaepernick jersey. That's what's up. Pleased to meet you, Ida.)

Ida:

Igualmente. Gracias por el cumplido. Lo apoyas a pesar de que estas en el ejercito. Eso es lo que pasa. (Likewise. Thank you for the compliment. You support him even though you're in the military. That's what's up.)

Becky Lynn:

We support him 100 percent! What he's doing has absolutely nothing to do with the military. Trust me…Ida's taken a knee way more times than Colin Kaepernick *ever did!*

At this point, Ida sneezes in a cute little girlish way.

Ida:

Achoo!

Franklin:

Salud, Chiquita. ¿Estas cogiendo un resfriado? (Bless you, girl. Are you catching a cold?)

Ida:

Gracias, Papa grande, pero no, son solo mis alergias. (Thank you, big daddy, but no, it's just my allergies.)

Franklin:

De nada, es un placer. ¡Feliz cumpleanos! ¿Cuantos anos tienes hoy? (You're welcome, it's my pleasure. Happy Birthday! How old are you today?)

Ida:
Garcias. Tienes diez y ocho anos. (Thank you. I'm eighteen years old.)

Franklin:
¿Diez y ocho? (Eighteen?) ¡Felicitaciones! (Congratulations!) Es un placer conocerte a ambos. Mi hermano habla de ustedes todo el tiempo. (It's a pleasure to meet you both. My brother talks about you guys all the time.) He speaks very highly of you two. Tell me. Voy a una barbacoa en aproximadamente una hora. (I'm going to a barbecue in about an hour.) ¿Te gustaria venir conmigo? (Would you like to come along with me?) Te puedes relo jor al lado mio. (You can relax around me.)

Ida:
Yes. I'd love to go to a barbecue. But…I have a boyfriend…so…I can't.

Franklin:
¿Eres feliz con tu novio? ¿Como te trata tu novio? ¿El te merese? (Are you happy with your boyfriend? How does he treat you? Does he deserve to be with you?) Pensandolo bien, no vamos al cine! No respondas eso. Mantente fiel a tu novio…mucho respeto. Me gusta tu estilo. El es un tipo muy afortunado. (On second thought…don't answer that. Stay true to your boyfriend…much respect. I like your style. He's a very fortunate guy.)

Becky Lynn:
Hola! I speak a little Spanish, too. Oh, man! We love barbecue! (pause) We've heard nothing but great things about you, too! Zharquaviyont is very proud of you and all of your accomplishments. But he never told us that he had such a handsome brother!

As Franklin turns back toward Becky Lynn, he's held back for a second because Ida hasn't released his hand as of yet. Franklin nods slowly again. After they make eye contact Ida releases his hand. Franklin backs away and lifts his palms toward Ida and Becky Lynn and says with a chuckle:

So hey, I just finished catching up and playing some football with some of my cousins and I'm feeling dirty and smelly right now. (pause) So, I'm gonna go take a quick shower. You guys can sit here and wait for small-fry if you like. They should be here any minute now. Just make yourselves at home. Nice meeting you, Ida. (dramatic pause) You too, Betty.

Ida sits and crosses her legs immediately after Franklin finishes speaking.

Becky Lynn:
It was nice meeting you too, Franklin. You smell really good, by the way. *¿Adios!* Oh, and it's Becky…Becky Lynn. But you can call me Betty if you like.

Franklin says as he is leaving:
Take care.

Ida:
Uh, Betty…If you use nine English words and one Spanish word, you're not actually speaking Spanish…okay?

Becky Lynn takes a seat beside Ida. Becky Lynn and Ida whisper amongst themselves on the sofa for fif-

teen seconds after Franklin leaves. Becky Lynn gets up to follow Franklin and Ida pulls her arm, motioning for them to leave. Becky Lynn pulls away and motions for Ida to leave. After Ida leaves the scene, Becky Lynn follows Franklin. Fifteen more seconds pass. Ida returns, crosses the stage and exits through the same door as Becky Lynn and Franklin. Fifteen more seconds pass. Afterwards, Ida reappears and walks very quickly back across the stage to the front door, just as LuPearl is coming through.

Scene 5-LuPearl and Zharquaviyont Return

LuPearl:

Ida? *What are you doing in here?!* Franklin Potts?!! Get your butt out here, boy! Right now!

> **After five seconds pass, Franklin and Becky Lynn emerge...disheveled.**

LuPearl:

Oh, Lloyd! Lloyd, Lloyd, Lloyd. End it right now, Lloyd. Kill me right now!

Zharquaviyont enters the scene quickly, carrying groceries bags, speaking as he enters.

Zharquaviyont:

Momma...what's wrong? (pause) WTF?

Ida with her palms up at her waist, facing LuPearl:

Miss LuPearl, I can explain everything. *I can explain everything.* This isn't what it looks like.

Becky Lynn:

Ida, shut up. This doesn't concern you!

LuPearl:

Becky Lynn, get back in there and fix your clothes! Franklin, you stay right there while I decide whether or not to take your life! Zharquavi-yont...lock that door. Ain't nobody leaving here until we get to the bottom of this. Ida, call your parents over here. Becky Lynn, call your mother! Tell her to come over here right now! Now Ida, what's going on here?

Franklin:

Momma, I can explain.

LuPearl:

Shut up! If you say another word...if you make a sound...I'm gonna choke the life outta you. You've got two choices, boy, silence or violence!

Becky Lynn returns to the scene.

LuPearl:

Becky Lynn, what's goin' on here? (five-second pause) Nobody wants to talk, huh? Well, somebody is gonna tell me something, one way or another. Boy, I've told you, until I was blue in the face, that one day, one of these little pee-smellin' girls was gonna get you into a world of trouble. And here it is. Just young, dumb and full of...

LuPearl jumps onto Franklin's back and puts him into a chokehold.

Ida:

I'll tell you what happened! Let me tell you what happened...please? Please let him go.

LuPearl releases Franklin, slinging him to the floor.

LuPearl smooths her clothes down and says:

Now we're getting somewhere. *Now we're getting somewhere.*

There is a knock at the door.

LuPearl:

Franklin, get your behind up and go put your shirt on! Zharquavi-yont...answer the door.

Becky Lynn's mother, Paula, enters the scene. Becky Lynn walks across to her.

Paula:

Becky Lynn, what's going on here? What's the matter? (pause) LuPearl (pause), what's goin' on here?!

LuPearl:

Come on in, Paula. We were just about to find out. Ida here was just about to tell us. Now Ida, I know that you're gonna be very honest with me right now, because I hate for someone to lie to me more than anything. I tend to get very upset and offensive toward people like that. Alright?!

Ida:

Yes, ma'am.

Becky Lynn:

Ida, keep your mouth shut! She lying!

Paula:

You keep your mouth shut. (pause) Well, Ida…tell us what happened. What's this all about?

Ida, toward Becky Lynn and then toward LuPearl:

Becky Lynn, I'm sorry. But Ms. LuPearl, this is the truth. This is what actually happened. Becky Lynn and I came over here so that she could apologize to Qua-Qua but he wasn't here. That's when Franklin answered the door. He said that he'd been playing football and was feeling dirty and was going to go take a shower and that she and I could *wait here* for the two of you to get back. That's when he left to go take his shower.

Zharquaviyont:

Ida, we don't need to know every little detail of what happened. Just get to the main part.

LuPearl:

You need to close your mouth. I need to know everything that went on in my house…every little detail.

Paula:

I agree. Go on, Ida.

Ida:

Well…Becky Lynn wanted us to go and peak in on him in the shower. I told her that we should leave and come back later. When I pretended to leave, she went deeper into the house. I followed her and hid in Qua-Qua's room, across the hall from the bathroom. I could see and hear everything from the closet. That's when Franklin said, "Is someone there?"

Zharquaviyont:

You went into my room?!

LuPearl:

Zharquaviyont, hush! Stop interrupting! (pause) Go on, Ida.

Ida:

Becky Lynn undressed and pulled the shower curtain back. Franklin was like, "Hey! What are you doing?! Get out of here!" And then she said, "Don't be embarrassed. You don't have *anything* to be embarrassed about, trust me. *I'm feeling dirty, too.* Is there room for one more?"

Ida:

Franklin said, *"Little girl, this isn't funny! Get the hell out of here!"*

Per Ida, Becky Lynn said:

"I'm not a little girl and I've never found a guy that didn't enjoy it as much as me. I hope you don't think that I'm fast or slutty because I'm not. At least *I* don't consider myself to be."

Zharquaviyont:

Every little detail really isn't necessary, Ida.

LuPearl:

Zharquaviyont!

Paula:

Out with it, Ida! What happened after that?

Ida:

Franklin got out of the shower, wrapped a towel around himself and said, "Little girl, you need to go. This isn't funny." She said, "I don't know why I'm even acting like this. I guess it's just because I'm curious about what kinda lover you'd make, or at least what you can do! Which I'm sure is a lot."

LuPearl:

And then what?

Ida:

Franklin came out of the bathroom and into Qua's room. Becky Lynn followed him and said, "Am I not appealing to you?!" And when she started twerking in front of him...Franklin got angry and yelled, "Get out!!" And she said, "Okay! Just kiss me and I'll go." She pulled at his towel and tried to kiss him and he pushed her away. That's when the towel came off and she knelt down and began performing fellatio on him.

LuPearl:

Fellatio? Now what is fellatio? What is that?

Zharquaviyont huddles with LuPearl and Paula and tells them what the word "fellatio" means. They react in shock and embarrassment.

Paula:

And what is twerking? On second thought, don't tell me. I don't think I need to hear any more. Becky Lynn, is this true?! Is she telling the truth? (pause) Answer me! Is this true?!

Ida:

I know that she and I may not be friends anymore after this but I have to do the right thing. And Miss Paula, Miss LuPearl…I'm telling you the truth.

Paula:

Is that it? Is that all of it?

Ida:

Basically?

LuPearl:

Well, get on with it. I need to hear everything. Put all the cards on the table.

Ida:

That's when I was able to sneak out of the room without them seeing me. I was about to leave when I met you at the front door.

LuPearl:

What were you here to apologize for? Why were you here, in my house, without adult supervision in the first place?!

Ida:

Becky Lynn told Zharquaviyont a secret and she didn't get the response that she'd hoped for.

LuPearl:

And what was the secret?

Ida:

I'm sorry, Miss LuPearl, but you'll have to ask her that question.

LuPearl:

Becky Lynn?

Paula:

Answer her question. Everyone's gonna find out soon enough.

Becky Lynn pauses for three:

I made a mistake with a guy because I thought that he cared about me…
and…I got pregnant. But he didn't care about me. He just wanted a
piece of my body.

Zharquaviyont:

What?! *You didn't tell me that!* Momma…she didn't tell me that she was
pregnant. She told me that she wanted us to take our relationship to
the next level. That's what she told *me*.

Franklin:

You're pregnant?!

LuPearl:

It just keeps going deeper and deeper. What else is there? I don't know
how much more I can take. Paula, did you know about that? Did you
know that your daughter was pregnant?

Paula:

Yes. I've known about it from the beginning. But there's no innocent party here today, LuPearl, and we all know it. Let's stay focused on the here and now if we could. Ida, why did you stay in the closet like a peeping Thomasina instead of trying to stop them?

Ida:

I'd rather not say.

LuPearl:

You'd rather not say?! Little girl, I've tried to be as patient and as peaceful as I could be. Get to the bottom of this so that I can do what needs to be done here. *Why were you even in the closet?* Why didn't you come out of the closet before all this happened?

Ida reluctantly says:

Because I enjoyed watching them.

LuPearl:

Claude, have mercy! *These kids nowadays!* They'll do and say *anything!* How much worse can it get?

Ida:

Ms. LuPearl, I'm so very sorry for being in your house without you being here. May I please use the ladies room?

LuPearl:

Go ahead. You know where they are. I feel sorry for your parents out there thinking their kids are walking around quoting scripture all day.

Everywhere they turn, they see *something sexual.* We just came from the grocery store and every magazine had either, a half-naked woman, a half-naked man or a now famous unwed teen mother on the cover. TV, movies, and honey, the award shows?! It's gone way too far, below the standard to turn it around! I need to call the police.

Paula:

LuPearl, meaning no disrespect, and I understand why you're upset. But I feel that I need to interject something here. I've listened, intently, to everything you've said and I've been able to follow your thoughts. But I'm not sure of what you're trying to say. Now, for our generation…this is very intense material we're covering. But to our kids…this is normal.

LuPearl:

So just what are you trying to say, Paula?

Paula:

I'm not trying to say anything. I'm telling you that even though breakdown of the family unit, violence in the home, teen pregnancy, multiple sex partners, sex before marriage and homosexuality happen daily in our world, there are still kids out there who walk the path of righteousness in spite of it. And they should be acknowledged. You've talked as if this is what every teen is doing and it is just accepted that this is how it is and it's just not true.

LuPearl:

Paula, I know that not all teenagers are out there conducting themselves that way. I'm trying to address the situation we have before us right here and right now. I've never said…what does that have to do with the situation?!

Paula:

My daughter, Nicole, is a prime example of what I mean. Somehow, she became the exact opposite of me. I'm sure that there are people out there who doubt that she's even related to me. She tells me all the time that a relationship with Christ is the only way for horrible, life-changing decisions to be broken.

LuPearl:

What does that have to do with what we're dealing with right now, Paula?! That's your problem...not mine! I'm trying to deal with mine!

Becky Lynn:

This is not about Nicole, Mom! Everything doesn't always have to be about Nicole! I get so sick of hearing her say that "the wages of sin is death." If she were here now she'd say, "Jesus is the Way, the Truth and the Life," and that what we're doing goes against what is taught in the Bible.

Paula:

You're angry with your sister for the same reason that I am. Deep down inside, you know she's right. She'll be the first one to break our family cycle.

The telephone rings and Franklin answers it. It's his Aunt Rosie.

Franklin:

Hello? (pause) Yes, ma'am. (pause) No, ma'am. Donovan hasn't made it yet and I haven't heard from him. I'm in the middle of something right now, Aunt Rosie, and I may not be able to make it to the barbecue. (pause) Yes, ma'am, I know. I'm sorry. (pause) No, ma'am. It's nothing like that. Everything's alright. I just can't make it. Tell everyone that I'll see them tomorrow at the church. No, ma'am, Momma and Zharquaviyont are gonna ride with me. (pause) Yes, ma'am. I love you, too. (pause) Oh, you're outside right now? Why didn't you just knock on the door and come inside? (pause) Aunt Rosie, there's no need to be that way. Stay where you are. I'm on my way out there.

Zharquaviyont:

Hold up! You're already pregnant and you tried to *get* with me?! And then when I turned you down, you went and had sex with *my brother under my Momma's roof?* How could you disrespect my Momma's house like that?! And Franklin, you must be outta your damned mind! Becky Lynn, we are no longer friends. And you need to leave.

Becky Lynn:

Yeah, I did it. And I'd do it again! I saw a chance at something good and I jumped on it.

> **LuPearl appears to be upset and slowly approaches Becky Lynn. Paula steps in between them in order to protect her daughter.**

Paula:

Now Becky Lynn, we're not gonna be disrespectful. Let's just go. We don't need to make things any worse than they already are. LuPearl, what my daughter tried to do here was absolutely wrong. I'm truly sorry for this turmoil in your home. I'd already put her on the pill. I don't know what could've happened!

Becky Lynn:
I'm not gonna be like you, Mom. I'm gonna find someone to be this baby's daddy. Adoption and abortion are out of the question. And Qua-Qua, if we are no longer friends, after all we've been through…then I'm cool with that, too. It's whatever. But just know that you're a very special person.

Zharquaviyont:
Becky Lynn, I really don't want to hear it.

Becky Lynn:
I'd just like to say I'm sorry. I said many things I didn't mean. Truthfully…everything I said…I didn't mean. I was upset and took it out on you. Please forgive me. If I die tomorrow…I'll feel a lot better about this chapter of my life because I've admitted I was wrong. On top of that I've asked your forgiveness. And Ida, this isn't over.

Zharquaviyont:
It's over, alright. Oh, you can bess believe it's over. If Ida would've stayed quiet, or not followed you, how long would you have carried out this little charade, up until the baby was born? Was that your plan? And I guess Detroit is the father, right?

Becky Lynn just nods her head yes.

Zharquaviyont:
I knew it. Why would you consent to having unprotected sex with a

fool who already has two kids by two different other girls anyway? *Common sense!*

LuPearl:

Now Zharquaviyont...*that ain't none of your business.* You've already said more than you should have.

Zharquaviyont says to Franklin as he inserts his earbuds in order to escape into his music:
And don't you even *look* at me!

LuPearl:
Detroit? Is that his real name?

Becky Lynn:
No. I don't think that's his real name.
LuPearl:
You don't think? *Well, what is his real name?*

Becky Lynn:
He just wanted me to call him "Detroit." This is gonna sound bad but...he looked good on paper...nice car, nice clothes...nice body... cash-flasher. I never knew his real name. He just wanted me to call him "Detroit" even when he was living with us for those few months.

LuPearl:
You're carrying his child and you don't even know his real name?

Becky Lynn:
Ms. LuPearl, I know what you must think of me. But where guys are

concerned, I'm all talk. I don't screw every guy I talk to. I'm not a stupid eighteen-year-old sex freak. I have pride. I like guys but not just to have sex with. I like to get to know who I'm talking to. I like for him to like me for myself and not for what I have. I actually thought that Detroit cared about me. But he just wanted a piece of my body and a place to stay. He got what he wanted and went back to his baby's momma. And yes, I was a virgin when I met him, in case you were wondering.

Paula:
LuPearl, now that everything is all sorted out, I'm gonna take Becky Lynn on home. She and I need to have a long one-on-one talk. Again, I'm deeply sorry about all of this.

LuPearl:
Paula, I need to say something to both you and your daughter. Now, I don't want any further hard feelings between us but Becky Lynn is no longer welcomed here. After this, she can't set foot in my house.

Paula:
LuPearl, I don't blame you one bit. I'd feel the exact same way. (pause) Becky Lynn, let's go.

Becky Lynn:
This isn't how the story ends, you know. I'm gonna be rich and famous one day. My baby and I are gonna be on TV. If other girls can become rich and famous for having a baby, then why can't I?

Paula:
Becky Lynn, don't embarrass yourself any more than you already have. Let's just go home.

Paula and Becky Lynn move toward the exit. Becky Lynn exits. Paula is about to make a startling confession. In the short time that "Detroit" lived with them, both she and her daughter were impregnated by him.

Paula:

LuPearl, this whole thing is my fault. This whole thing could have been avoided if only I had been a better example for her to follow. My daughter and I are both pregnant and without husbands. The father of her baby is the father of my baby, too. A person has to get creative when they're alone and still have the desire. I'm so very sorry. This is *all* my fault.

LuPearl:

Paula, far be it from me to judge you…and not to give too much business but in my culture, we as black women will run a good man off by wanting to be his "supreme ruler." *We do it better than anybody.* That was me *up and down.* I "supreme ruled" my way into two divorces.

Paula:

Wouldn't that all depend on what kinda man you're with, though? If the man is not willing to be trained, then maybe it's best to give him his walkin' papers. Well, I guess it's like my old Uncle Rupert used to say. "It takes love from a man to keep his woman but it takes respect from a woman in order to keep her man." Old Uncle Rupert may have been right.

LuPearl:

*And then to top it all off…*I got involved with a man half my age. I was thirty-seven. He was twenty. Half of the blame here belongs to me. But our children *don't have to make the same mistakes we made.* Some can learn the easy way but some have to learn the hard way. Goodbye, Paula.

Paula:

Bye, LuPearl. I have something to do in the morning but I'll see you at the church for the funeral. How long do y'all's funerals usually last? (pause) Well, nevermind. I'll just see you over there after I'm done, alright?

> **Paula goes to the door and exits the scene as Ida returns simultaneously. Zharquaviyont removes his earbuds as Ida approaches him.**

LuPearl:

Ida, why haven't your parents made it over here yet?

Ida:

They're all down at the police station.

Zharquaviyont:

The police station?! What happened?!

Ida:

My sister's new fiancé, Dexter, got into it with her "baby's daddy," Erasmo, at our house during my niece's birthday party. Erasmo showed up *uninvited and smelling like weed.* My dad and brothers got involved and one of our neighbors called the police. This kind of thing has never, ever happened in my family before.

Zharquaviyont:
Didn't she already get an injunction or a restraining order against him?

Ida:
No. Not yet. She filed. It's just taking some time. My mom said that it all started when my niece, Jasmine, was seated at the table about to blow out her candles and Erasmo stood her up in the chair. She blew out the candles and kept standing. So, Dexter told her to sit down before she fell and she did. Erasmo didn't like another dude telling his daughter what to do and it was on from there...*a melee at my parents' house. This kind of thing has never, ever happened in my family.*

LuPearl:
That's how it is nowadays. When your sister's fiancé proposed...he made a commitment to not only accept her and her baby. He agreed to accept the "baby daddy," too! Somewhere along the way, the old-fashioned "package deal" was changed to include the sperm donor. It's changed, I'm tellin' you the truth.

Ida:
Ms. LuPearl, I think that I'd better go.

LuPearl:
Ida...thank you for speaking up and doing the right thing here today. It took a lot of courage to do that. Very few people would've had the courage. Now, you're not guilty of anything but you're not welcomed in my house either...at least not until I speak to your mother. For now, let's just say goodnight and leave it at that. Have your mother to call me as soon as she gets back, if you would, please. She and I need to talk.

Ida:

Yes, ma'am. I'll tell her. Goodnight, everyone. Again, I'm really sorry.

Ida exits the scene as LuPearl opens the door. As she exits Franklin allows her to pass and then re-enters through the doorway.

Scene 6-The Aftermath

LuPearl takes a deep breath and says:
I don't even want to know why she called you out to her car instead of knocking on the door and coming inside. I don't know and don't care. She's silly and all of her sisters are silly.

Franklin:
I didn't choose the Potts' to be my family, Momma…you did.

LuPearl:
Franklin, you just dodged another bullet. Another crisis averted, as you would say. You stood right there (pause) and told me that you'd cut out all foolishness. You have embarrassed me and brought shame on this house. I've never been ashamed of one of my children before. You're throwing your military career away! Are you hell-bent on throwing your life away, too?

Franklin:
No, ma'am.

LuPearl:

I can't tell, boy. I can't tell. You are about to graduate from military college, commissioned as a Second Lieutenant, with no student loans to pay back and a job, of your choosing, waiting for you.

Franklin:

It was just a moment of weakness, Momma.

LuPearl:

All it would take is a moment of weakness, Franklin!!! It was a stupid decision! You have a genius-level IQ but you make stupid decisions! What good can come from a genius making stupid-ass decisions?!

Zharquaviyont steps in between his brother and mother and says simultaneously:

Please, Momma...calm down before you get your blood pressure up. Franklin...do you see what you've done? Do you see?! Maybe you should leave, too...and never come back.

Franklin to LuPearl simultaneously:

None, Momma.

LuPearl:

That's right, boy! None! You lied to me! I'm very disappointed in you, Franklin! And even more ashamed! Even with military training, you still lack discipline. It was all for nothing. You're a liar. God only knows what else you've been lying about.

Franklin:

I didn't lie, Momma. I'll prove it to you. From now on, there'll be no more involvement, or any kind, until my wedding night. Momma, I put that on everything I love. Without you, I never would've accomplished anything. I'm gonna make you proud of me again, Momma. Just give me that chance.

LuPearl sits down and begins to cry.

Zharquaviyont immediately rushes over to comfort his mother: Don't cry, Momma. Do you see what you did now, Franklin? Do you see?! Just leave. Just go.

LuPearl appears to be exhausted. She collects herself and says:

After I die, it is my greatest wish that either an angel in Heaven or a demon in Hell will pull me aside and explain to me why you did the things you did. Then maybe…I'll understand. I had…such high hopes for you. But…I couldn't teach you how to be a man. Boys, I'm very tired. I don't know how much more I can take. We've got your father's funeral in the morning and I'm going to go on up to bed. You two can… go to bed, stay up, leave or whatever.

Franklin, wiping away tears: I'm sorry, Momma. Momma, I'm sorry. I love you, Momma.

LuPearl stands, exits the scene silently via the stairs and does not respond. Zharquaviyont turns and heads for the front door after receiving a text message.

Franklin:

And just where did you think you were going...sir?

Zharquaviyont:

None of your business! (pause) But if you must know, I just got a text from Becky Lynn. She said that if it's a boy, she's gonna name him Royce and it it's a girl she's gonna name her Saiyah or maybe Zamoria. Her mom revealed to her that "Detroit" is the father of her baby, too. She suspected that anyway. I'm just going over there to check on her.

Franklin:

That would've been very considerate of you. But the only checking that'll be done tonight will be me checking to see whether or not you're in there snoring. Go to bed or "knuckle-up and let's throw them thangs." No one is leaving here tonight!

Zharquaviyont:

And who are you? You don't tell me where I can or can't go. You ain't my Daddy!

Zharquaviyont snaps his fingers and heads for the front door. As he approaches it Franklin says:

If you *touch* that doorknob...this conversation is gonna take a really... really ugly turn.

Zharquaviyont:

So you think that you can give me orders now?!

Franklin:

That's right! Let me explain something. That woman up there is no longer proud of me. And as far as I'm concerned, I'd rather be dead. (pause) So you see. There's about to be some immediate changes. I'm going to do whatever it takes to regain her trust. That also means that I'm going to be the big brother that I should've been years ago. I wasn't here when your father committed suicide at your little sister's funeral. I wasn't here when you were molested by Aunt Opal. But I'm here now! And I'm not going anywhere, because I love you!

Zharquaviyont:

Not as much as I love you. But why didn't you come to my hair show?! And you know that those are sensitive subjects. *Don't play with me like that.*

Franklin:

I'm not playing. I'm as serious as a heart attack. Now, I'm sorry that I didn't make it to your hair show. But I have two brothers and no sisters. The time has come for you to stop acting like a girl. I know that you've had some struggles. *Everyone has struggles!* You're not a girl, Zharquaviyont! Stop acting like one! (pause) After my graduation, I get to my first duty station. You're coming with me. You're gonna go to school. You're gonna get a part-time job and you're gonna get a girlfriend. It's time to grow up!

Zharquaviyont:

A girlfriend?! Are you crazy? I don't even like girls. You can't just snap your fingers and change my lifestyle. You don't have any idea what it's like to live the life! *I'm not going anywhere with you! And keep your voice down before you wake up my Momma!*

Franklin:

She's my Momma, too. You remember that. You know what...I'm ac-tually *done with the conversation.* Momma wants her children under this roof and you're not going anywhere tonight! Tomorrow night you can do whatever. But tonight...you're going to bed. You, Momma and Do-novan are all that I have. And that's all I have to say! Goodnight, love ya. See you in the morning. (pause) Let me come in there and find you're not in bed and see what happens.

Zharquaviyont:

Whatever, Franklin.

Franklin:

Listen to me and use your brain for a change. If you live up to one of the many stereotypes perpetuated against us, it is no longer a stereo-type. It becomes an accurate observation. Let that bounce around inside of your head. (five-second pause) Hey, have you heard from Donovan?

Zharquaviyont:

Not since he called earlier. But I think Momma talked to him a little while ago. Why don't you just call him since you want to speak with him so badly?

Franklin takes a blanket from the sofa and prepares to sleep in front of the front door:

Night-night...sleep tightcha and don't let the bedbugs bitecha.

Zharquaviyont:

You do know that that's not the only way out...don't you?

Franklin:

Of course I know that. But you won't be leaving through this door. You'd better not leave through any door. Leave this house and see what happens. I'm done. **Franklin puts up a peace sign sideways and says:** Peace to you and peace on you.

Zharquaviyont turns out the lights. The stage is dark for approximately thirty seconds in order to show a new day has begun. When the lights come up again, the family is preparing to go to the funeral. LuPearl comes out in a beautiful purple dress with gold accents, then Franklin in full uniform, and finally Zharquaviyont, dressed in a black perfectly tailored man's suit. The telephone rings and Zharquaviyont answers it. Franklin assists him with his fits from head to toe, starting with his tie.

Closing Scene

The family has gathered around the table to partake in the massive breakfast that Franklin has prepared. Pancakes, maple sausage, a large bowl of smoking-hot maple syrup, both pork and turkey bacon, grits, biscuits and gravy, hash browns, scrambled eggs with cheese, cinnamon toast, hot coffee and cold apple juice.

Zharquaviyont:

Hello? (pause) Oh, hi, Miss Rosie. (pause) Yes, ma'am, we're just about to leave right now. (pause) Yes, ma'am, he's here. Hold on for a second. Franklin…telephone.

Franklin takes the phone.

Franklin:

Yes, ma'am. (pause) No, ma'am. You don't have to send the limo over here to pick me up. I'm gonna ride with my family. We'll see you at the church. (pause) Okay, Aunt Rosie. Yes, ma'am, I'm sure. Bye.

Franklin hangs up the phone and says:
Momma, that reminds of something I want to ask you.

LuPearl:
What is it?

Franklin:
If I'm assigned to Korea after graduation, I'd like for you and Zharqua-viyont to come and live with me. Would you consider moving to Korea together…I mean us as a family?

Zharquaviyont:
Ain't nobody movin' to Korea with you, fool. I don't know anybody in Korea! I don't even know where Korea even is!

Franklin:
That's something that you should've kept to yourself. Being this deep into the information age, there is absolutely no reason, whatsoever, that you shouldn't know where Korea is located. OR at the very least be able to locate it on an atlas. There's no excuse for that level of ignorance. Momma…would you consider renting the house out or maybe selling it outright in order to come with me to Korea?

LuPearl:
Sell my house? Boy, please.

Zharquaviyont:
See there. I tried to tell you. Ain't nobody trying to follow your buttocks to Korea, or anywhere else for that matter. And don't think that I didn't hear your little ignorance comment. I'm gonna let that slide. Don't be

callin' me ignorant.

Franklin:

It's a good thing that the final decision isn't up to you, small-fry. Momma has the final say. Momma…I know that it's a major decision but would you at least think about it…please?

LuPearl:

I'm not making any promise but I guess that I can give it some thought. I'll pray about it. But that's all that I can promise right now. Mount up and let's move it on out to the church.

Zharquaviyont:

Momma…you don't have to try to spare his little feelings. Just tell him right now. We're not moving anywhere.

Franklin pulls an envelope from his jacket pocket and says:
Here you go, Momma. I brought you a little dust up here. I forgot to give it to you during all of the commotion last night.

LuPearl:

Commotion caused by you! **Franklin hands the envelope to LuPearl.** Now what is this?

Franklin:

It's $800, Momma. I'll have two more for you after the funeral. I've just got to get by an ATM.

LuPearl:

Here. Take it back and let's go. There's no tellin' where or who you got this money from.

Franklin:

Take it back?! Momma, you are still adding to your retirement fund, aren't you?

LuPearl:

No, I am not. I stopped that almost a year ago. I don't care about savin' money no mo...no mo! I've already told Donovan not to send me anymore money and now I'm tellin' you.

Franklin:

A year ago?! Are you serious?! "Everybody needs a nest egg." That's what you said. *That's what you taught all three of us!* You're gonna need that retirement money, Momma.

LuPearl:

But when I die...*look at all of that money somebody else is gonna spend.*

Franklin:

Momma, you're not making any sense. You're going back on something you've taught us? Zharquaviyont, did you know about this? Why didn't you tell me about this?

Zharquaviyont:

No, no, no! I'm not in it! Momma and I already had this conversation. Keep my name outcha mouth, sugar-booger!

LuPearl:

Franklin, this matter is closed. I don't want to talk about it anymore. Take this money and don't say another word about it.

She gives the money back to Franklin and he accepts it.

Franklin:
But Momma…

LuPearl:
Silence or violence, Franklin…silence or violence?

Franklin:
Momma, you're gonna take this money…and you won't even know that you took it. Yes, ma'am.

LuPearl:
I don't want to have to wrinkle my clothes up before I get to the church but say something else. *Say one more word.* (pause) *Make a sound.*

Franklin:
I love you, Momma.

LuPearl:
Immm hmmm. Not as much as I love you, baby…not as much as I love you.

Zharquaviyont:
You don't have to say another word to me either but I'll take that 800.

The curtain closes and the stage goes black.

The curtain reopens for the introduction of the cast of characters.